STORIES OF EX[illegible] AFRICA

PAUL OLSON

EDITED BY MARGIE WARNER OLSON AND JOYCE DANIELSON

outskirts press

Nestlings
Stories of Expatriate Life in Africa
All Rights Reserved.
Copyright © 2020 Paul Olson
v3.0

This is a work of fiction. Names, characters, businesses, places, events, locales, and incidents are either the products of the author's imagination or used in a fictitious manner. Any resemblance to actual persons, living or dead, or actual events is purely coincidental.

The opinions expressed in this manuscript are solely the opinions of the author and do not represent the opinions or thoughts of the publisher. The author has represented and warranted full ownership and/or legal right to publish all the materials in this book.

This book may not be reproduced, transmitted, or stored in whole or in part by any means, including graphic, electronic, or mechanical without the express written consent of the publisher except in the case of brief quotations embodied in critical articles and reviews.

Outskirts Press, Inc.
http://www.outskirtspress.com

ISBN: 978-1-9772-3074-4

Cover Image by Margaret Olson

Outskirts Press and the "OP" logo are trademarks belonging to Outskirts Press, Inc.

PRINTED IN THE UNITED STATES OF AMERICA

To my beloved partner Paul,
Who calmed the storm in me
And showed me the world.

CONTENTS

FOREWORD

All of the short stories in this collection are works of fiction. They are set overseas in places where Paul either lived or traveled. Each story contains some elements of real events he experienced or heard about. The first story, "Nestlings," is set in the Ubangi region in what is now the Democratic Republic of Congo (DRC), where Paul attended a mission boarding school during second grade. The next three stories, "The Freezer," "On the Rocks," and "Great Barrier Reef," all took place in Somalia, where Paul and I worked in the mid-1980s at the American School of Mogadishu. At the time, the country was a military dictatorship under President Mohamed Siad Barre. It was relatively stable and received financial, economic, and military support from the United States and other Western powers. "The Freezer" is a reimagining of a true story Paul was told when visiting a friend who worked for the UN in the northern city of Burao. In "On the Rocks," the ship that ran aground in the port was a real event that dominated everyone's life and attention for several weeks. In

"Great Barrier Reef," Paul shares his love of fishing off the Somali Coast in a boat he owned and rebuilt with several friends.

The final story, "Breakfast in Bali," was written in 1995 after our family's evacuation from Rwanda in April 1994. We had been working at Kigali International School in Rwanda for two years, during which time the country had become increasingly less stable. We had just returned from a long Easter weekend trip to a safari park near the town of Goma, DRC, when the genocide began. Once back in the United States, Paul followed the news of the genocide and its aftermath relentlessly, as it affected (and still affects) the entire region of Eastern Congo. Of all the characters in these stories, it is through Walt that Paul comes closest to expressing his own moral dilemmas with pacifism and living in Africa as a person of privilege.

Each story contains a few words in the indigenous or colonial languages of the countries where the stories are set. These languages include Lingala, French, Arabic, Somali, Italian, Kinyarwanda, and Balinese.

Finally, none of the characters depicted here are real people.

Margie Warner Olson

All proceeds from the sale of *Nestlings* will be donated to Education Congo, an organization that provides support for several universities in DRC as well as scholarships to Congolese university students. Before his illness, Paul was a member of the Education Congo board of directors. For more information, go to www.educationcongo.org.

Front cover: The author, about age five, holding a weaver bird nest at Wasolo, Ubangi Province, DRC. Photo by Clitus Olson

NESTLINGS

Uncle Roland told the children he had angel wings. Tommy studied the tight smile on his lips. He liked Uncle Roland because of all his jokes, but for once he wanted to believe him. In those days, ever since he had come to the dorm, Tommy had wanted to see an angel. Uncle Roland joked about angel wings just before Tommy's father gave him some shots around the mole on his back. Uncle Roland wanted to show that shots didn't hurt, so he let the kids stay in the bedroom of the guest house and watch. Tommy's father was getting ready to cut out the mole, and he didn't want the kids in the room for that, so he shooed them out. Just as they were leaving, Uncle Roland wiggled his bare shoulder blades at them: "See? Wings!"

All the uncles and aunties were gathered at Karawa for the Christmas program. Afterward, they would take their children back to their own mission stations for vacation. The missionaries were not really relatives, but they had decided among themselves that it was a good thing to encourage this family feeling since they were all so far away from home. Tommy's mother and father had come late the night before in the blue Ford pickup from Kala. It was so late they weren't going to wake him up, but like his roommates, Benny and Ricky, he was wide awake, and he knew the truck by the sound of it as it labored up the hill. He had run through the big living room of the old house in his pajamas and out the door in his bare feet, the screen door slamming shut behind him. The big kids laughed, but he didn't care. He ran up the dark palm lane without a flashlight and didn't even stub his toes. The Ford's headlights were still beaming in the drive of the guest house when he got there. In a second he was high in the air looking into his father's smiling face. Then, his mother took him away and hugged him. There wasn't enough room at the guest house, so he had to go back to the dorm for the night. This was the rule: all the kids had to stay in the dorm until vacation started.

In the afternoon, the classes went up to the big house at the head of the palm lane to practice for the Christmas program. It was dress rehearsal, and the big boys were teasing the little ones about picking at their baggy shorts when they stood to sing on the steps of Old Main. They said when Tommy picked at the edges of his shorts it looked like a dress. He didn't want to look like a girl—neither did Benny or Ricky. Claude couldn't help what he did. If he tried hard and pulled his thumb out of this mouth, he would put his hand on his wiener, just like a village boy. The big boys thought this was even funnier.

Miss Johnson told them all to quiet down. Then she said, "Take a deep breath."

The little kids' choir sang their song over again. This was the song that would come at the end of the program, after the big kids had done their play about Mary and the baby Jesus.

Old Main was the biggest house on the station. It had a wide veranda all along the front that made a perfect stage, and the steps leading up to it were just right for the choir. Its roof was thatched with *sobi* grass, and for the program, they had tied more *sobi* to the brick pillars to make it look like the barn for the manger scene. The houseboys were working out on the lawn unfolding chairs for the audience.

At the end of the dress rehearsal Miss Johnson smiled her peppy smile and said to them all, "Tonight there will be music under the stars!"

One of the big boys snorted, just loud enough so she could hear. It made her cheeks blush a little under her blue winged glasses. The big boys were always saying mean things about Miss Johnson, but Tommy liked her. He and Benny thought she was pretty, no matter what the big boys said.

After rehearsal, Tommy ran down to the guest house with Benny and Ricky flanking him. Benny's parents were there too, but Ricky's still hadn't come. Uncle Roland was out on the porch with Ruthie and Auntie Elaine. Ruthie was the best one in their class, and she was showing her report card to her mom. Tommy skidded to a stop on the porch, caught Uncle Roland's eyes, and wiggled his shoulder blades at him. Uncle Roland smiled back, but Auntie Elaine looked off to the palm lane, trying to ignore him. She didn't think Tommy was funny, and she wanted him to know he was interfering with family time.

He ran on down to his parents' room.

His mother was saying, "You've done all you can."

His father mumbled to her in a hurry, "It's pretty grave." Then he called out, "Hey there, buddy!"

Tommy pulled his report card out of the thick brown envelope and handed it to his mother. His father moved over by the bed to read it with them. He bumped the bundle of mosquito netting with his head, and it swung gently over the bed like a puff of cloud.

The word "grave" filled Tommy with a sad feeling like homesickness. Katherine, one of the big girls, had read him a story about a grave one night at the dorm. It was in *Life* magazine. You got to see America in *Life* magazine. A little boy and girl had been kidnapped. Their mom and dad waited for a long time to pay a ransom, but no ransom note came. Then, seven months later, an old man walking with a cane accidentally poked a hole in their shallow grave in a park. There was a picture of the grave covered with lots of dark, wet, autumn leaves. The two children looked out of their pictures straight at Tommy. "So sweet," Katherine had said of them. That night at devotions, Uncle Roland had asked the children again if any of them wanted to be saved. They were singing, "There Is a Green Hill Far Away," stringing out the words, "so dearly, dearly," until Tommy thought he would cry. He wondered if he was saved. Since he had come to the dorm, he had found out that some of the kids hadn't been saved yet. He'd always thought he was, but now he wasn't so sure.

"Let's see what you've learned, young man," his father said, peering down his glasses at the report card. "Pretty good in reading, I see." That was for the B.

"Looks like you're having a little trouble in arithmetic."

"A C means I'm doing OK," he told his father. "Miss Johnson says so."

Only Claude had flunked, and he couldn't help it. Miss Johnson had said that too.

"Yes, a C is just fine," his mother said.

She gave his father one of her looks.

Then his father asked, "Well, what else have you learned this school term?"

There was a lot he had learned that he did not want to tell. He couldn't tell about the big boys and their snapping towels, for instance.

"For Cub Scouts Uncle Roland taught us how to make traps. Ricky and me caught us a stink rat!"

His parents laughed gently. He tried to think of more that he would be able to tell them.

"I learned to draw."

"I just knew you'd be good at drawing, dear," his mother said.

He stood quietly, unable to think of anything else to say. His father stood up, ready to go somewhere, and his mother moved over to the desk.

"We're so proud of you, Tommy," his mother said. "Here, draw me something."

She handed him a sheet of white stationery from the

desk where she had been writing letters most of the day for the mail truck. It was supposed to come that day with presents from America.

Tommy spread the paper on the cool cement floor and started to draw with a pencil. His parents whispered for a while by the desk, and then his father said he would go back down to the hospital.

Tommy hadn't wanted to tell them that he had been looking for angels. Nor did he want to tell them what he had learned about baby birds, or about the spooky snail's sound. But, because Uncle Roland had even brought a snail back from a Big Sunday, maybe he could tell them about the snail. In the village, Tommy had heard it make its humming sound—a long, dreary moan—all night long. The next morning, when he asked the villagers about it, they brought him one. Maybe not the one he had heard, but one like it. It was as big as Tommy's shoe and had dark brown stripes with yellowish ones in between. The villagers said it made its sound from a hole in its neck just behind the feelers. Nobody at the dorm could see the hole, but maybe that was because the snail was always pulling itself inside its shell. And at the dorm, it never made its sound, so Uncle Roland let the houseboys have it because they liked to eat that kind of snail. All the kids said they had heard at least one of those snails moan out in the *zamba*. Sometimes, late at night, when the generator was off, you'd think you were hearing a truck, like the mail truck, moaning up the dirt road across the valley. It would moan and moan, like some ghost or *ndoki*, but never come. Once, Tommy heard one two nights in a row. It started up the second night about where it had left off the night before. Even just last night, Tommy thought he'd heard it, just before he heard the Ford.

Now, angels were something else. He'd been keeping his eyes open for them for some time. He hadn't seen one yet, so he didn't want to tell his mom and dad, because if you really had seen one, you surely must be saved. You couldn't say you hadn't seen one if you'd been trying, could you? Because then maybe it meant you hadn't been saved after all. Tommy wasn't too sure about all this, so it was better to just keep quiet in the meantime. On his paper, a stick figure grew wings—thin, see-through ones like termite wings with tiny veins. On another, he tried to make a lot of feathers, more like bird wings.

At devotions he had asked about angels. Had Uncle Roland ever seen one? Two of the big boys, Dickey and Bobby, snickered, but Uncle Roland gave them a frown. No, he hadn't, he'd said, but he hoped to one day in this life. Certainly, he would see them in Heaven. Uncle Roland asked the kids sitting around the circle if anybody had seen one. Nobody raised a hand, but then Norma, one of the big girls, said she hadn't seen one, but she'd felt one standing beside her sometimes. Dickey snorted, but Uncle Roland stopped him and said he'd felt angels watching over him, too. Auntie Lina nodded, and so did some of the other kids. From then on Tommy had wanted to see an angel himself—really see one for sure. Maybe you had to look really hard, with your eyes wide open like the village boys did when they were hunting with slingshots. They could see a bird in the thickest bunch of leaves or catch sight of one out of the corner of their eyes almost like magic. Tommy kept his eyes open.

He had asked Mike, one of the nicer big boys, about it. They were out on the veranda of the dorm on a Saturday morning shelling peanuts. Each student had to shell a cup of peanuts before playing. This was a rule and a good one. Each Saturday the houseboys cranked peanut butter out of the meat grinder to fill a couple of mason jars. It was just enough peanut butter to last for the week.

Mike popped open a shell over his cup thoughtfully and answered Tommy's question, "Seeing angels? I don't know. Maybe it's more like sensing them."

There were all kinds of senses, Mike explained. Like the way his dog, Tippy, could sense when she was going to have her puppies, and she would always go to the same special place each time. Instead of having them in his bed, she would go to his sister's bed. Maybe she could sense she was a she. Then there was the way a hunter could sense his prey, and the prey could sense the hunter. Praying mantises were sensing all the time, the way they moved their green shoulders back and forth with their eyes spread out wide. Bats could sense their way in the dark—maybe not fruit bats, because they were big and clumsy, dropping mangos all over the place—but the little bats that squeaked in the dark could sense their way. It was a kind of radar.

"Is it like arithmetic?" Tommy had asked. "When you know your pluses and minuses by heart and somebody asks you, you just sense the answer?"

"Yeah, I guess it's like that, too. People are smarter

than animals. We can sense a lot more things. It's one reason why we can tell we have a soul."

Tommy sat there on the veranda trying to sense all the things he might sense. Maybe he could sense where the birds would hide in the *zamba*, the little patch of jungle next to the mission. Maybe, if he tried hard enough, he could sense where the *simbiliki* rats were running in their rumbles through the tall *sobi* grass. There was a cloud growing out over the valley and he watched it as he shelled the peanuts. He could sense it growing out there in the bright blue air, all white and mounding out. He got a sense of faces showing there: noses and chins and foreheads. But one thing he could sense for sure was that it was getting itself ready to rain.

"That cloud is going to rain at two o'clock this afternoon."

Mike made a snort and said, "How do you know? You can't hardly even tell time yet."

"But I know," Tommy said. "I can sense it."

Tommy studied the picture he was drawing of angels. The one with the feather wings didn't look right. It looked more like a beggar loaded down with a sack of sticks. He scratched them both out, rubbing the pencil point down flat.

"Mom, can you sharpen my pencil?"

She was busy writing, but she stopped and took it.

"Here," she said. "Take this one. Now, show me what you've done."

"It wasn't any good. I need another paper."

"Let's not waste paper, Tommy," she said as she pulled

one out of a little stack on the desk. "I don't have much stationery left."

He looked at her desk. There was a neat pile of letters in blue envelopes. His mother had written boldly over them, repeating what was already printed there: *Par Avion*/Air Mail. She always wrote this on both sides to make sure they got on the DC-6. The mail truck would take the letters to the airport at Libenge. Other letters from his grandparents and the Sears Roebuck catalog had told her Christmas presents would be coming by sea. They were too heavy to come by plane. Those presents would take the train to Leopoldville. Then they would take the river boat up to Businga. The mail truck was to bring them the rest of the way. She had been praying they would come today, on time, but it was already getting late in the afternoon.

Maybe the truck knew Tommy had done something wrong. Like Santa, it wouldn't want to bring any presents this year because Tommy had kept the baby birds: tiny baby *ndele-ndeles*. He had stolen them, nest and all. Ricky had warned him that if you touched the birds their mother would never take them back. Even touching the nest might drive her way. Once you touched them you had to take care of them, or they would die.

He'd found the nest in a grapefruit tree. The mother *ndele-ndele* kept flying up into the leaves carrying things in her beak. She was tiny, black on her head and shoulders, with a white bib. For a week he had watched her come and go, listening to the thrum of her wings, then the trill of her babies deep in the nest of pale grass. Their cries sounded like a small rattle gourd when it was shaken softly. He waited so that the babies could get bigger and become easier for him to feed. But then, he couldn't wait any longer, so he poked the nest out of the tree with a broomstick. This was during siesta, when nobody could see him. He had simply walked outside minding his own business like he was going to the outdoor toilet behind the cookhouse. Like all *ndele-ndele* nests, it was thick, round, and soft, with a small hole for a door. Grass seeds on it made it smell like freshly baked bread. The babies landed safely, so he hurried back into the dorm with the hall echoing faintly of the sound of the rattle gourd.

Ricky and Benny kept the secret. They had an eye dropper to feed the birds milk. You were allowed to take milk from the kerosene refrigerator anytime, even though only a few kids could stand it because it was lumpy powdered milk. Bread was harder to get. Tommy brought back an extra slice from the table for crumbs. There was a rule: no pets. And another: don't waste food. He had to watch carefully at the table before he snuck a slice of bread into his shorts.

The baby *ndele-ndeles* were neat. They had pert little heads with baby feathers sticking out of them like tiny porcupine quills. Around the edges of their beaks they still had milk marks. Their backs and bellies were bare-skinned. Wings poked out of their backs like tiny elbows with only a few quills for fingers. They spread them when they begged for food, which was all the time. Their hot bellies seemed full enough. You could see their guts wound up in there, blue and pink and purple against the clear skin. But their cries now seemed less like a rattle gourd, because you could hear each little voice.

Tommy found excuses to run back to the dorm at recess to feed them. The boys fed them during siesta time, when they should have been resting. That was another rule they were breaking, and it was Tommy's fault. The birds woke up after supper when the boys turned on the light. They fed them to keep them quiet. During devotions Tommy heard them when everyone was quiet in between prayers, so he had to hope the grown-ups wouldn't notice. One night, just to help out, Ricky requested a favorite song as a hidden prayer for the birds: "Children of the heavenly Father, safely in his bosom gather. Nestling bird nor star in Heaven, such a refuge e'er was given."

But the birds were not getting enough food during the day. Their cries got weaker. One wouldn't hold its head up for food. Benny force-fed it with the dropper, and it drowned. That left three.

They wanted to bury it, but they couldn't let anyone see them. Benny said they could give it a funeral in the outdoor toilet. Ricky said the prayer, asking for forgiveness, especially for Tommy who had taken the bird from its mother in the first place. Tommy dropped it down the hole.

The next morning there had been two more to drop down. Later, at night, they snuck the nest out with them and dropped it down with the last dead one in it. Nobody wanted to shine the flashlight down the hole.

Now Tommy wondered if he was ruining everyone's Christmas. He drew the mail truck with Santa riding high up on the back frame.

His mother pulled a rubber band around her pack of letters. She looked down at his picture and gave him a hug. A warm tear splashed on his knee.

"Santa will come, Tommy. I just know he will."

Tommy didn't like to look at his mother when she cried.

"Come on. Let's go over to Old Main. I need to put these in the mailbag."

They walked out into the bright sunlight of the late afternoon. In a little while Tommy would need to get down to the dorm for supper. Then he would need to shower and get dressed for the program.

At Old Main his mother talked with the other aunties. Auntie Elaine had been crying, too. They were all talking about the DC-6. Someone said it was lucky that Elaine and Roland could catch tomorrow's flight. Auntie Lina said it wasn't luck at all, it was God's hand. Tommy's mother leaned over and whispered that Ruthie and her parents were going to get to fly home to America for Christmas. Tommy looked at Ruthie leaning her head on Auntie Elaine's hip, and he could tell she didn't feel this was so lucky for them at all.

Just then, down at the bottom of the palm lane, the dorm kids started to jump and yell. The mail truck heaved its mass into sight above the *sobi* grass and groaned on up the hill. The kids chased it wildly up the palm lane. The older boys jumped on its running boards, while their mothers looked at them aghast. Then the ladies hurried down the steps of Old Main to meet the truck as it pulled to a stop in the shade of the large mango tree.

The boy chauffeur didn't have a chance to do his job. The big boys were already in the back tossing out canvas mail bags that bulged with boxes inside. Their fathers joined them. On the red dirt of the palm lane, the women wrestled with the bags, pulling at the knots to break the blood-red sealing wax that bound them. The little kids collected pieces of sealing wax from the ground to trade later. From inside the bags, their fathers' muffled voices called out family names to announce the boxes they were finding. Their big grown-up butts were in the air, but nobody seemed to mind because, suddenly, everybody was unbelievable happy. There would be plenty of presents to take home for Christmas.

Tommy's mother hugged him. Even though there were tears in her eyes, she was smiling like this was the best thing that had ever happened in the world.

"This is going to be the best Christmas yet," she promised him.

It made supper late at the dorm, but that was OK. The houseboys heated extra water for showers, filling the shower buckets as fast as they sprinkled empty. Everybody got dressed up in their white shirts and blouses, dark pants and skirts. When they were all ready, they gathered on the veranda. Each big kid was paired with a little one. Katherine, the big girl who liked to read to Tommy, held his hand. The children walked up the palm lane in the dark in two rows, Uncle Kurt and Auntie Lina showing the way with flashlights.

"This was like walking in the ruins of the Temple of Karnac at night," Katherine whispered to Tommy. "Look how the palms raise tall pillars to the temple roof, where the stars can peek through the fronds up there."

Katherine got to be Mary. For the baby Jesus, she held a real baby in her lap, Benny's new sister. Dickey got to be Joseph. Some of the big girls were wise men and shepherds because there weren't enough big boys. The big kids said all their words just right. They ended their part singing songs in harmony, with Mike and Dickey doing bass.

Then, the little kids filed up the steps to sing. Tommy took his place in the top row and looked out over the choir to the audience. Flashbulbs were flashing like giant stars popping against the dark of the palm lane. Miss Johnson raised her arms, and the children's heads all turned to her. She mouthed, "Take a deep breath." They kept their hands to their sides, perfectly. Tommy did not touch his pants. Then, they breathed out their song. Surely, they were being turned into angels in their parents' eyes, for all the "oohs" and "aahs" in all the mouths out there. Shoulder blades beat with each verse. Beneath white blouses and shirts, bare-skinned baby bird wings sprouted into angel wings that spread wide, opening out in all that flashing glory.

THE FREEZER

This happened back when I took a surveying job overseas, thinking I'd get a jump on the game making all that extra dough. You got an overseas bonus, and it was all tax free. You didn't make as much as you could in Saudi, but you saved more than you ever could surveying in the Emirates. I was fresh off of a stint with the Army Corps of Engineers, so I figured I could handle a real adventure. And I did. But I guess I wasn't so ready. I still can't get over how I ran out on Ned, even though I think he'd understand why I did it.

Magens, our company, sent Ned Hollings and me up to Burao in northern Somalia to do a route survey for a new highway. This was before anybody knew where Somalia was located, a few years before Bush sent in troops to try to straighten out the place. Ned and I were teamed up with a local contractor, Abdi Noor, whose crew was supposed to do the preliminary bladework and gravel base. The problem was half of the time the grader broke down, or the driver was out sick from staying up late chewing khat, or Somalia was having another fuel shortage. Our work was supposed to take six months. Then, Magens was sending in the rest of the team to lay down hardtop across that desert plateau.

Imagine a highway for camel herders and wandering nomads, people who, for thousands of years, had set their course to thunderheads on the horizon, hoping the next growth of grass would show there. All you could see was this flat plain slanting up to a few desert mountains. Behind them, it broke down in an escarpment that overlooked the Gulf of Aden. There weren't any wild animals, just camels and cows and goats: big African adventure! Those herdsmen out in the desert looked more like something out of the Bible than Africa.

The highway would link Hargeisa and Erigavo in the North with Mogadishu way down South to promote unity—which was a joke, because people in the North had been waging a guerrilla war for years. The word was out to leave us alone. I guess both sides figured the highway would be useful when they finally got control of the place. Once in a while we'd come across a huddle of rebels hiding in ambush down a dry wash, and they'd wave us on. We'd play dumb, like you were supposed to do if you were a foreigner, and we didn't ever say anything to the soldiers at the next roadblock. Politics.

Ned and I were sent to Burao to start the roadwork. It was hardly even a town. We could only get camel and goat to eat in Burao, and African beer. If we wanted anything that seemed like home, we had to make a trip to Berbera and bring it back to Burao. Berbera—about eighty-five rough, hot miles away—had the only other Americans around. They were building up the pier on the Gulf so that our navy ships could use the place. Those guys had it made with a pool and satellite TV. MAC flights brought them T-bones, Doritos, ice cream, beer, anything. Their compound was a regular piece of the States.

There were about a dozen foreigners in Burao: Ned and me, some Pakistanis, Germans, and Chinese. We were all tied up in development projects, mostly agriculture and medicine. Not that the Somalis had any use for agricultural advice. They'd been herding for thousands of years and didn't give a damn if some expert thought the place was overgrazed. As for the hospital, it was a place they went to die. Who needed Chinese acupuncture to speed things up? Somalis went straight to the little pharmacy by the market and bought their own antibiotics, or they just stuck to their medicine men, the sheikhs. What they wanted were guns to fight each other with, and none of the donor countries would give them any—not the clans, anyway, though we gave plenty to the central government to face off the Cubans next door in Ethiopia.

One of my first days in Burao I took a walk down to the market in the middle of town. Noisy, dusty place. Thorn trees, donkeys, camels, loads of people, but man, did they make a point of ignoring me. To them I was just an infidel. I bought a pack of cigarettes at a little stall and headed on back toward our place. Then this little old sheikh came walking alongside me. He had on this dinner jacket over a white shirt and flowing robes around his legs, had a silver grip on his walking stick, and he wore a white turban. Somalis wear those Arab skullcaps, *kofias*, and this guy did, but you don't see a lot of them with turbans wrapped around them like he had. His beard was salt and pepper with a tinge of red henna at the tips from his last trip to Mecca. He started talking in pretty good English and he mumbled something like, "You tell your embassy people in Mogadishu they send more guns, lot of guns. Tell them with your radio." Then he kept strolling along as if he were walking by himself, gradually passing me by. It was like something out of a bad spy novel: just ask and it will be given. That's what you get in a country run on a donor economy. As Ned would say, Somalia was a real basket case—all basket and no bread.

Magens set us up in one of the best European houses in town, with four bedrooms, Italian tiled floors, a musty refrigerator that wouldn't set Jell-O, a freezer that actually worked and, would you believe, air conditioners. The appliances were nearly useless, though, because the town generator only ran for four hours at night, and only when there was enough diesel.

Magens was too cheap to buy us a backup generator for the house, which is what got to Ned most, because it made the landlord's freezer real touchy. It was ancient already, and with all the revving up and shutting down of the generator Ned was sure the freezer would blow. He'd sit there listening to it hum. Then it would rumble up to an active rattle, a rattle that would ding and sniffle with every fluctuation of the town's tricky generator. With those tile floors and no curtains, each ping and pop would ricochet all over the place. Drove Ned nuts.

He set up rules for opening it. We could lift the lid

once, but not too high, when we got home from work. This was to pull out a couple of six-packs which, with any luck, would still be half frozen, and we'd take out a package of meat for supper too. New beers went into the freezer at the same time. Then we'd have to wait for four hours while the generator ran the freezer before Ned would let me open it for a few more cold ones before we hit the sack. Ned refused to let Hassan, our cook, open the freezer, ever.

"Open it any more than that and the meat will rot," Ned would say. "All we need is to get food poisoning in this dust bowl."

Not that Hassan was too excited by what we kept in there anyway. As a strict Muslim he wouldn't even touch alcohol, and anything that looked like pork gave him the shivers.

Ned wouldn't touch camel meat. Down in the market they hung it out in the open air, brown stuff just shiny blue with flies and smelling wicked rancid. For Ned it had to be the steaks we got from the Seabees in Berbera, the more freezer burned the better. We got all our meat and beer from them even though they weren't supposed to let us have any, government regs and all. These guys could see we needed it, and the extra cash was good for their card games.

Ned had been to all kinds of places for Magens, so he had these special rules for survival—hardship post survival, he called it. He'd always say, "You gotta watch your ass in places like this." This meant you basically stuck to your work, followed clean habits like washing your hands and feet regularly, boiled your drinking water, stayed with your own kind, and never lost your temper with the locals, or they'd sabotage your work. Basically, you kept yourself out of trouble. Not that there was a lot of trouble to get into out there. Ned said the Somalis would kill you if you touched their women, and the only drug they were into was khat— which on my first try, was a little like chewing coca leaves, but it only gave me a buzz like sour coffee.

There was one restaurant on the edge of town. We called it the Goat Restaurant because that was all you could get there: whole goat roasted on a spit and stuffed with cardamom rice and dates. There was a cinder block kitchen and a half-dozen thorn trees with tables under them. They let us bring our beers there and we'd eat under these strings of colored light bulbs and the stars. Sometimes the Germans would come with us and we'd gab the evening away. But you can only eat goat meat so often. Most of the time we just ate at the house.

That was our life. We'd work, sweat, and bake all day in the sun, then lick the dust off our teeth in the evening for that first frosty brew from the freezer and kill some time reading spy novels, waiting for Hassan to cook up the steaks.

When I first got to Burao I tried to be sociable with Ned. I'd sit near him after supper and make conversation. I hadn't been in a hardship post before, but I figured at least we could keep each other company. And I needed his advice. He indulged me in the beginning, but it soon became clear that Ned had other interests. So I dug into my spy novels. Ned would get on the shortwave radio and make the evening call down to the office in Mog. Then he'd listen to AFRTS out of Germany, keeping abreast of all the sports. He'd put his feet up, and you'd think he was watching the games on TV, but we didn't have one. I don't care much for sports, but I thought I'd get something going if we bet on a few games. Well, Ned wasn't into gambling either and he said so. He said he was saving his money for retirement. That was his reason for being in Burao for six months. He had plans. So I put on my Walkman and played music loud to block out the sound of the sportscaster's voice. Then I'd read my books.

Lonely is a word I'll always connect with Burao. Sometimes I'd walk over to the Germans' place down the block. The three of them had a big TV and a VCR with lots of tapes of soccer games to watch. That didn't interest me too much, but I would hang around just for the company. The tapes came up from their Mog office, and they each took turns going down there on business. They always had news of the great parties people were having, and any new women that showed up at the Hash.

The Hash was this sort of combination fun run and fox hunt on foot with a beer bash at the end. It was something bored colonials thought up out in Asia. I got in on a couple when we first got in country. Great place to meet just about everybody in the expat community, including the few single women down there in Mog. Great way to see the countryside too. Saturday afternoons you'd go out to a designated spot where a trail had been set. Then, you'd run around with everybody looking for the trail, trying not to be misled by offshoots, yelling "On, on!" if you thought you were on the right track. Others would come trailing after you through the dunes, dodging the wait-a-bit bushes and thorn trees. One Hash was on the sand dunes above Shark's Bay. It ended on the beach with everybody arm in arm around a campfire, doing "Down, downs," the chugging required of winners, losers, and basically everyone for some made up reason. Up in Burao, it did my heart good just to hear about the Hash from those guys.

I guess you could say that our social equivalent was the dirt tennis court where a couple of the Germans and Pakistanis would play Ibrahim, the governor of Burao. It was a dirt court built with the net set up in-line with one of the many local anthills. A nice columnar anthill, about ten feet high with smooth notches up near the top, made a perfect throne for a referee to sit. They dug a couple of steps for climbing to the seat. The governor had a four-foot-high wall built to surround the court, and street kids made a great business of ball chasing whenever anyone had a match. A little whitewash for the court lines now and then and you had tennis. At one point the Germans got some extension cords and lights, and had the kids shimmy up the trees and tie the lights in them for night games, but one light got stolen early on. So the regular game time got to be the beginning of the cool, just before sunset. I don't play too well, myself, but they got me to be the ref often enough. At least it was something to do.

The governor, Ibrahim, was from a clan in the South—the president's, no doubt. He'd gotten a college degree at Michigan State back in the seventies. Both these things made him as much of an outsider in Burao as the rest of us foreigners. He and Jurgen, a German, were the tennis champs. They were serious players and once they'd get going, you'd hear Ibrahim start to get American.

"Shit!" he'd yell. "That one was good, Mike, you motherfucker!" with his wiseass grin, so proud of his vocabulary.

Jurgen would egg him on, "You'll never beat McEnroe."

"Shut the fuck up and serve, you motherfucking motherfucker!"

The ball would whiz past Ibrahim, bounce over the mud wall, and he'd yell something in Somali to the street kids who were scrambling after it, ending with a couple more of his obscenities. There must still be people in Burao proud of the special American vocabulary they learned from Ibrahim.

Afterward, we'd go over to the Germans' place and have a few beers. Ibrahim would talk up East Lansing like it was the greatest place on Earth: the leaves in the fall, football games, hot dogs, the snow in the winter, and all those American girls.

"Jah, and where are they now?" Jurgen would kid him. Gradually we'd all drift back home for the night.

Late at night, with the town quiet, you could hear guns from time to time: artillery duels with the Ethiopian backed rebels across the border. It scared me the first time and I wondered what I'd gotten myself into. I asked Ned the next day if he'd heard it, and he said he had.

"It's just between them, Mike," he said. "Don't worry."

Ned told me he'd worked contract in lots of places where there had been penny-ante civil wars like this. They were always too busy fighting each other to bother with foreigners. "But, hey! This is what bumps up our pay. It's not just the dust we're dealing with, Mike. It's the danger. Plus, if things ever really do heat up, Magens will take care of us. They'll see we get evacuated, pronto."

That's one of the reasons why Magens kept radio contact with us. Not all that reassuring, if you ask me. But after we came across some of those rebels in dry washes who just let us pass by, I began to believe Ned. "They could take us hostage anytime they want, you know," he had said, as we drove down to Berbera on a beer run. "But they don't, so I figure we're all right." For all its logic, this kind of reasoning didn't do me any good late at night when the guns boomed, like faint thunder from sheet lightning, just over the horizon.

Every other week Ned needed a haircut. He showed me how he liked his butch: red and bristly, so short you could see the skin on top, which was easy anyway because it was pretty thinned out. I let him cut mine once a month, to ease his mind. It just drove him crazy to see my hair all sweaty and wet, sticking to the back of my neck. "Like spaghetti," he'd say.

Ned was all cleanliness and efficiency. Up at the crack of dawn, shower and shave, ready to go. He treated the work like some military operation, and I knew I had to pass inspection. I shaved, too. I wanted to make a good impression on him. My chances for any good-paying hardship stints in the future depended on it.

The road grader kept breaking down. At first Ned went crazy over it because each time it set us back a week. The contractor, Abdi Noor, said he didn't have any way he could get parts quickly, so we got them. We'd radio down to Mog for them and wait for the office to ship them up on the next weekly flight of the little Fokker Friendship, a tiny turboprop that could only carry small pieces of equipment. Sometimes the office had to get the parts sent by DHL out of Europe, which then took another week.

What was supposed to take us six months was looking more like a year. Ned was itching to retire. He figured six months would put the icing on the cake for him, but the more things got delayed, the more he tried to resign himself to it. A guy like that doesn't resign to stuff without a bit of awkwardness.

"It'll put me into a new boat," he'd say, trying to convince himself.

His wife was already living in their retirement bungalow down in St. Pete, and now he could see a bigger boat out in the marina, outfitted to charter for sport fishing. Each week he'd read her new letter over and over. It'd be full of stuff about their grown kids: two daughters and a son. Almost more important, she'd tell him about the house. He'd write her back, reminding her about stuff to do for the garden or around the house.

"She'd better get somebody to service the air conditioner before it starts to get too hot. It's March already, for shit's sake." He'd hand me a snapshot of the backyard that she'd sent him. "I wish she'd get a gardener to come in and lay some new sod over that dead spot."

Crazy shit like that. You'd think he was living there already. Man, he could get antsy over it sometimes.

I couldn't stand sitting around the place when the blade was down and Ned was bitching away. Why should I even stay? It was just so stupid and boring. Ned didn't like it when I'd start to rant and rave. He was a little afraid I'd quit. Then where would that leave him with the project?

"Hey, Mike," he'd say to me. "You're packing it away. Even while you sit here on your ass, you're getting paid. It all adds up. When you get back, you'll have the dough. I wish I'd started saving it as young as you. I'd be out fishing right now."

Ned had done twenty years with the Corps of Engineers before he'd come over to Magens, but the pension just wasn't enough for him.

"Hell," I'd say. "This isn't worth any kind of money. Not this sitting around in Burao all day, no air conditioning in this heat. Open the windows and the dust blows in."

"It'll be worth it when you get home. The girls go for a guy with a lot of dough."

"Who says I want any girl like that?"

"Oh, you'll want one soon enough," he'd say.

After a while, when it looked like we'd be off a week, and I'd been moaning and groaning around the place too long, Ned would send me down to Berbera on a beer run. He wanted me to catch some snappers off the pier while I was at it. Take an extra day, since we wouldn't be able to do much until the blade got fixed.

By then, the soldiers at the roadblocks knew me to the point where they'd just salute me through. Made me feel a little like I was running the Wells Fargo stage, driving my pickup down Sheikh Pass, which looks a lot like those desert mountains in old cowboy movies. One time I saw a couple of ostriches running along in the flat country down next to the sea. That time it really felt like I was in Africa. Ned didn't need to go himself, but made it clear he didn't expect me to hurry back. Ned was thoughtful that way. He took an interest and sometimes I felt like he was treating me as if I were his son.

This had its downside. He hardly talked about his own kids. It seemed they weren't close. Once in a while I'd be listening to ZZ Top or Springsteen on my Walkman and he'd walk through the room shaking his head to the hiss of it, mouthing words at me. Same kind of stuff my old man used to say, like, "How can you listen to that shit?"

Ned knew Burao was a bad place for me, but he tried to show me the best of it. That always came back to the money. Made me kind of sick to keep hearing about it: how he wanted me to have his kind of success, only earlier and smarter. But for a while there, I thought I wanted it too. He would get friendlier, open up a bit more at night.

I don't know if this was out of desperation to make me stay on the job with him, or if he actually had begun to like me.

I know I began to like him. His cranky remarks about Somalis always ended with a gentle, forced smile. There was humor in this, and he used it as another survival tactic. He didn't really dislike the Somalis; they were just a handy target for his anger. I was the only one to hear those jokes. He was a good model for dealing with the locals because he showed them nothing but patience. "You won't get anywhere in these places with a bad temper," he'd say, after outwardly showing calm in accepting the contractor's latest news of a breakdown.

But Ned wasn't always so cool and patient as he let on. The delays wore on him in ways that worried me a little. He had a habit of putting his hand to his gut after a meal and making a show of pressing it to let out a loud burp. It was a corny kind of show like he probably used to put on for his kids when they were little. Now, it was just bachelor's manners. But it wasn't so funny when he'd forget to play the cornball routine. He'd squint his eyes like he was trying to feel where the bubble was in his stomach, but he couldn't quite find it. I figured it was more than indigestion, and I finally came out with it. Well, he didn't think it was anything to worry about. Back in St. Pete he'd have them check him out. He wouldn't take any pressuring from me to go down to Mog and see somebody, so I just left it at that. He probably knew what was best for himself anyway. And what was best for both of us was to get this damn job over with.

Finally, it looked like we were making progress. We'd gotten extra spare parts, enough to get us through about three breakdowns, and we had a stock of fifty barrels of diesel. But then, the blade itself cracked in the middle. We scrounged around town for a welding machine, but the only one we found was broken. We radioed down for another one, but our office wasn't sure if they could find a spare one in the country. Might take a while. Abdi Noor, whose business it was to take care of his own damn equipment anyway, just shrugged his shoulders and spread his hands wide: "*Inshallah*," (God willing). Typical Somali attitude!

I figured the guys down in Berbera had to have plenty of welders to spare, extra metal to reinforce the blade and whatnot. Ned nodded, "Good thinking, Mike." That night he got on the radio to them and described the situation. They said, "Sure, haul the thing on down." We dismantled the blade next morning, Ned doing his best to be patient with the Somalis as they tussled in more of a tug-of-war than an actual lift to get it onto the back of the pickup. Then we had to figure out the best way to let it ride so it wouldn't get ripped apart any further from bouncing down the road. Got some old crates under the blade and bound it tight with a bunch of bungee cords. Its ends stretched out over the sides of the bed like stubby little wings, and I headed on down Sheikh Pass dreaming I could soar off the escarpment catching enough thermals to carry me on a long glide down to Berbera.

Well, the Seabees were willing to be of help when I pulled into their compound, but there was an obligation that came first: their own orders. They had forgotten to mention that, right then, they had their welding equipment, complete with a generator, way the hell out on the pier binding up reinforcing rod, and there was a lot of cement they had to lay around it, fast, before the southern monsoon really started to kick up the water.

"But you guys said over the radio—"

"Yeah, somebody talked too free, and the colonel overheard it. No way he wants the work slowed down for nothing."

"I could drive the truck on out there, just for a little while, you know. Just need a couple of spots; wouldn't take too long."

"Hey, that thing needs a lot more than a couple of spot welds. When and if we get the chance, we'll do it up right. We've got all sorts of scrap to really shore it up. But that's going to have to be a couple of days from now. Sorry."

I called Ned that night over their radio. He groaned and asked how long it might take. When I told him, he just said, "Well, why don't you catch us some fish while you're at it? I'm getting tired of these steaks." We agreed I'd radio him each night, just in case the guys eased up and got the job done sooner.

There were some Filipinos working contract with the Seabees, and they had the fishing all figured out. You could catch just about anything right off the pier on a hand line, but the biggest things were sharks—plenty of them. You used monofilament about as thick as clothesline, and you wore gloves.

I hooked into one five-footer, probably a mako, though nobody knew for sure. Everybody cussed and laughed whenever I got pulled over to where they were trying to work on the pier. Called me "Lady and the Tramp" because I was skipping daintily along that cracked old pier like I had a strong dog on a leash. I wasn't exactly excited about getting pulled in, and it took me three hours to get the shark up. But it was a great way to forget about my troubles with the blade. After that I concentrated on the snappers because they were really tasty. There were pink ones, red ones, and gray ones. I loaded up on them, keeping out of the Seabees' way, and got the cook to freeze them up in the walk-in so I could take them back to Burao in my cooler.

Best thing was I caught up on American TV, hours and hours of it: Johnny Carson for breakfast, Donohue for a midnight snack and, praise be the big satellite eye in the sky, the Playboy Channel for siesta. This was the life! To hell with working for Magens! I wanted to get with a company that had contracts with these guys.

On the third night down there, Ned didn't call in. I blew it off as him relaxing a bit, because the night before I'd told him it would be at least another four days. The next morning, I didn't feel right about him missing the call, so I tried to radio him, but he was out, of course, probably finding some sort of work to keep himself busy. That night he called at the regular time and apologized for not calling the night before. He'd been sick, he said. Today he'd gone over to see the Chinese doctor.

"Do you need me back there? I can blitz up first thing in the morning."

"Nah, don't bother. I'm better already. Have you caught any decent fish yet?"

"Yes, plenty. Snapper."

"Well, bring them on back with you after you get that blade fixed."

"Roger that."

"And out."

I had a hard time getting to sleep that night. Staying up late watching TV had gotten me jumbled up in my time zones. Finally, toward morning, I got in a few hours of fitful sleep.

I woke up nervous, jittery, a little hungover. I wanted to get back up to Burao, pronto. I got some guys to help me unload the blade, telling them to get to it as soon as they could. While they were working, I loaded up the cooler with snapper and ice and grabbed some beer and a whole carton of Doritos. When the blade was fixed and reloaded, I hauled ass up the escarpment and then on down the plateau into Burao. It was hot when I got there, late afternoon.

I stomped into the house and Hassan came into the living room, wearing shoes. He never wore shoes. The place was freezing, and the floor was all wet. The air conditioner was rumbling away, and it was the wrong time of day for that to happen.

"Where's Ned?"

"See Germani. You go to his house."

"I said, where's Ned?"

"You go now. Talk to Germani."

"No, not now," I said, and I headed for the kitchen, not liking what I was seeing.

The kitchen was a mess. Packages were piled in puddles on the floor. I got this crazy notion that the freezer had broken, and Hassan was trying to keep things cold with air-conditioning. He wouldn't touch alcohol, so he hadn't taken out the beer. I lifted the lid of the freezer.

The freezer was steaming cold. Ned was in there, up to his jowls in six-packs. His knees were up against his chest. He had this disgusted look on his face like he'd been stuck in there, trying to push his way out with his feet for hours. There was a ring of frost nestled in the red bristles on the top of his head where the lid had rested. I stopped my hand from reaching down to touch him. I almost said something to him but then couldn't find any words. The fog rolling around him said he was frozen solid.

Hassan leaned heavily on his mop handle as I came out of the kitchen. I headed straight for the front door.

"Governor make all time 'lectric for Ned. Make him ready for airplane."

I slammed the door on Hassan's words.

My passport was still in the truck and so was my suitcase and my Walkman. I scooped the snappers out of the cooler onto the ground and mashed a couple of six-packs in their place. Then I filled eight jerricans with diesel, using a hand pump on the supply barrels, and tied them down tight with bungee cords. Hassan watched all this banging around from the front door, slowly shaking his head and saying, "Ah, ah, ah." He steadied the mop handle by the door and started heading for Jurgen's house. I figured I could make Mog in eighteen hours if I drove straight through. Then, I could catch the Thursday plane out to Nairobi. Magens was going to have to send somebody up on the Fokker to pick up Ned, because I had just fucking quit.

On the Rocks

Soap bubbles spilled over the seawall and swirled across the port road with the opaque intensity of a blizzard. Cheryl Brown thought she had seen it all, but now a thirty-foot container of detergent had tumbled off the ship that had run aground in the harbor. The container lolled against the rocks, battered by the surf, and belched up bubbles like a washing machine gone berserk. Great drifts of foam pressed against the seawall, where the monsoon wind skimmed bubbles off their crests to spin shiny taffeta globes up the narrow alleys of the old Arab quarter of Mogadishu. Somali boys chased after the bubbles with the same glee that children chased after first snowflakes in Indiana. Cheryl's daughter, Mandy, let out a chirp of delight from the back seat.

For a moment, the mesmerizing flow and whirl touched the squalid seafront with a kind of magic that matched a tale Cheryl had heard of a Sufi holy man who had been shipwrecked on these shores hundreds of years back. Never wishing to step aboard another sickening dhow, he'd lived out his exile teaching in the mosque.

On the day of his imminent death, believers caught sight of him as he was spontaneously buoyed up by his prayer mat and borne away over the rooftops of the city toward Mecca.

Cheryl's husband, Andrew, eased the car gently off the tarmac and parked beside the seawall to view this latest episode in the ship's saga. He had loved the disaster from the start. Each day he would pick up Cheryl and Mandy from school, and they would stop at the port on their way home. First, there was simply this huge container ship, stories tall, looming above the town, foundering at the mouth of the new port, where a tug's rope had proven too weak against the broadsiding wind. Containers on deck mounted up to the sky, "like Babel," Andrew had first said. Atop them, Land Rovers and Mercedes teetered drunkenly. Fortunately for the town, its own goods had been offloaded in the port before the wreck—anything falling off the boat could be seen as fair game. Cheryl had watched with dread during the first week, when young Somalis began swimming out to grasp debris floating on the heavy, shark-haunted waves. The containers began to topple in ones and twos, to drift ashore and break open like giant Christmas presents filled with all manner of wealth from the far corners of the earth. Crowds clambered down the jagged, dark coral to fight and haggle over bright things, setting up a festive market on the spot. Andrew had joined a betting pool at the embassy over the fate of one silver Mercedes. He claimed it served as a pleasant diversion from the demands of his work, but he was still pretty upset when he lost by a margin of eighteen hours. In the end, his Mercedes couldn't float, so Cheryl reveled in the thought of lobsters and octopuses already well ensconced in its lavish interior down under the sea.

This storm of bubbles would fit quite well into Andrew's cocktail party canon of anecdotes, along with the other quirky details in his stories of foreign coups and famines and revolutions. It might even supersede the one about the woman in Guinea who had carried a pilfered porcelain bathtub away on her head. As Cheryl watched him gaze through the windshield at the bubbles it struck her, from the avid curiosity in his eyes, he felt above these events, as if he could always enjoy these disasters under a kind of private diplomatic immunity.

Mandy coughed in the back seat, a gagging cough at the ammonia smell that had begun to seep in through the air conditioner.

"Are you okay, Mandy?"

Mandy nodded bravely, her cough under control, but her eyes teared up in the effort.

"Let's get out of here, Andrew. This stuff is bothering her."

The smell mixed tartly with the stench of the fish market and the dirty salt air. It startled the nose. All three of them sneezed simultaneously. Andrew turned off the air conditioner and drove onto the road, moving slowly in poor visibility to avoid the boys darting through traffic.

The air cleared as they turned toward downtown and by the time they passed the embassy and USIS, there were only few bubbles in sight. They drove along the beach front that the Italians had optimistically called the Lido and continued on toward their home among the seaside houses of Embassy Row.

As they waited outside the metal gate for the guard to let them in, Andrew said, "I'm a little disappointed," as he edged into a lousy imitation of Lawrence Welk, "I so wanted a little champagne muzik mit doze bubbles fer our klassik Amerikan filum on zuh patio."

"You would," she said with her irritation showing.

After all, she would be the one busy that afternoon seeing to it that everything was ready for the film party. All she needed was a change of wind, loaded with bubbles, to chase the guests inside where they could spill drinks and smoke up the living room.

Once the car was inside the compound, Mandy fussed over her seat belt. Cheryl opened the back door and unfastened it for her. Mandy hurried under her arms to wriggle out of the seat as Cheryl reached for Mandy's lunch box and her own book bag. She doubted she would find time to correct papers, but taking the book bag home had become a habit. Out of the corner of her eye, she saw Mandy racing up the steps for her appointment with her grandmother's latest video. Andrew stepped into the garage to check the fuel gauge on the backup generator.

"At least the show will go on," he said, "even if city power goes down."

Lately, this was happening all too often, and the houses up and down the street had begun to grumble and hum almost nightly. Every other week a new generator would add its plaint to the chorus, as even the poorest of diplomatic missions imported private power sources.

"Let's go see how the gardener has set up the chairs this time," Andrew said with a smirk.

Cheryl walked with Andrew around the front of the house to the side patio where the film was to be shown. A few neem trees and stunted coconut palms sprouted up from prim holes in the cement to throw meagre circular shadows. Only the bougainvillea seemed to flourish against the compound wall. The chairs were ranged facing the high wall of the house where the picture would be projected. Next to the ranks of chairs, the portable bamboo and thatch tiki bar stood ready for action looking, for all the world, like it was on loan from the set of Gilligan's Island.

"Looks perfect," Cheryl said.

"I believe we've got this one trained."

"Be nice, Andrew."

"What would we do without him?"

"A little exercise wouldn't hurt you."

"Ha!"

Andrew set himself to straightening chairs anyway, to get the rows more perfectly aligned.

By the time Cheryl got in the house, Mandy was watching her new Sesame Street tape. Cheryl was allowing her one segment a day to stretch out the tape's value. She peeked in the den where Faduma, the *boyessa*, sat next to Mandy on the floor.

Faduma turned to smile reassuringly at Cheryl.

"Remember her bath, in half an hour," Cheryl said, pointing to the clock on the bookshelf.

Faduma nodded and turned back to the screen

where Big Bird bounced around to an alphabet letter song. She whispered into Mandy's ear, pointing at the screen as if she were teaching the girl. Mandy wiggled her shoulders.

"Shut up, Faduma. I'm trying to watch!"

Faduma sat back timidly and arranged her blue gauze shawl neatly over her shoulder. Mandy's insolence disturbed Cheryl. It was something that had only recently begun to surface.

"Mandy, that's not nice. You shouldn't talk to anybody that way. Tell Faduma you're sorry."

"But she keeps bothering me."

"She's only trying to help, sweetie."

"She can't turn on the video. She can't even read. All she does is bother me."

"Mandy, say you're sorry."

"Now you've wrecked the show, Mommy. I'm going to have to start it all over."

Cheryl raised her voice a notch. "Don't you start with me, Mandy. Say you're sorry."

Mandy mumbled, "Sorry" as she scrambled over to the VCR and jabbed the rewind button.

Cheryl hurried down the long hallway to the extra bedroom she used as her office. She dumped the book bag on her desk, took a quick look inside at the folder of papers her second graders had written, titled "My Best Day," and decided they could wait. This certainly wasn't one of her best days. She decided she'd be able to scan them the next day during recess, just before language arts. The film party would take up too much of her evening so, in the hour of

Mandy's video and bath, she deserved a little down time. But she needed to make a quick check on Abdullah in the kitchen first.

As she walked down the steps to the lower level where the dining room and kitchen adjoined a cavernous foyer, she hoped the damn bubbles would stay away.

Abdullah looked fully attentive to his tasks. *Sambusas* were frying in a huge pot, and he was busy slicing up carrots, arranging them on a silver platter among assorted finger foods.

"Everything okay, Abdullah?"

"Yes, Madame. Everything plenty fine."

She knew she irritated him with her presence. The kitchen was his territory, and it was hard for him to relinquish it. Even though he tried to be tactful, he never failed to fidget when she came in. But that was just too bad. He couldn't think of everything.

"Use the Saran Wrap tonight, Abdullah. Leave it on the plates until the guests arrive."

"Yes, yes, Madame. We keep flies off."

"And any of those blasted bubbles."

"Oh, yes, very bad. Radio he say maybe poison, stay away from ship."

"Really?"

"Not really really. Maybe really. But government mad because too many people stealing things, so he make them little scared."

"That's certainly useful information," she said. And manipulative, as always, typical of the regime. She would ask General Mahmoud about it at the party, diplomatically of course, not to ruffle his feathers. But she'd mention at least something of this.

Opening the fridge for a bottle of tonic and some ice for her glass, acting as if this were her reason for lingering, she wondered what Abdullah had lined up for their light supper. To the side of a plate of finger food, he'd set a bowl of salad made from the same ingredients but artfully cut in smaller bits. Then she peeked into the oven, nonchalantly, before she headed for the door. A small lasagna, one of his specialties, was warming for supper along with trays of *sambusas* and egg rolls.

In the living room, Cheryl pulled out a bottle of Boothe's Dry Gin from the liquor cabinet and fixed her drink. She picked up her latest *Architectural Digest* from the coffee table and stepped out the sliding doors to the wide balcony overlooking flat white rooftops and the sea. From here, one might be on the Cote d'Azur. This view always soothed her. There was the white line of the surf where the reef paralleled the beach, its sighs muffling the sounds of light traffic. The water inside the lagoon glowed a creamy blue in the late afternoon and, outside, the depths took on a darkening grade of blue to the eastern horizon. Tufts of low riding clouds were already shadowed in pewter and highlighted in rose by the sun setting over the continent. It was here that Cheryl collected herself for the coming frazzled hours at diplomatic receptions and dinner parties; here, she gathered around herself this luxurious calm, this beautiful evening air.

She watched the drift of the clouds for a moment to gauge their angle of approach to the shore. It seemed to her they were holding their usual course, and with it, a few miles south, the wind would carry those awful bubbles on a current well clear of her house. This comforted her, and she sat down in her deck chair to attend to her drink and her magazine.

Cheryl scanned the glossy photographs. Polished dark wood interiors set off exotic tables and over-stuffed chairs from the 18th century. Gilt framed mirrors reflected the rooms down to infinity, all grounded in sumptuous Oriental rugs. They mocked the embassy's regulation Ethan Allen fare that cluttered her monstrous house. No matter how she arranged their personal things—Andrew's collection of gigantic West African masks, her Haitian primitivist paintings and Guatemalan weavings, her baskets, the cluster of family photographs she'd enlarged and matted herself—she never could get them to fit the rangy, outsized floor-plans of the houses they'd been assigned. Yet the ornate rooms in the magazine could never be what she wanted either. They lifted up a dream of wealth and sophistication she had long abandoned. They reminded her of luxuries offered in a poem of Baudelaire's, "*L'Invitation au Voyage*," which had charmed her when Andrew and she had studied French together that year in DC, after he'd finished his master's degree at Georgetown. They were going to adventure together—armed with this French and his good scores on the Foreign Service Exam—on a diplomatic career taking them to the salons of world capitals and the distant islands of the French Commonwealth. But of course, they'd had to first take postings in francophone Africa, the hardship posts that earn you the privilege of a spot in Paris or Rome. Toss in Haiti, then Central America despite their lack of Spanish, and now Somalia, where Italian might best serve, and it was becoming clear that Paris remained far, far away.

Could it be that Andrew was a little too young? Other friends had already gotten there. More likely it was Andrew's closet liberalism, his caustic quips irrepressibly surfacing at the name of Ronald Reagan. Or was he harmed by his anecdotes of the humorous side of hardship posts? His superiors might find them slightly frivolous and befitting a man of little substance. He'd been told he was chosen for Somalia because of his superior adaptability to such crucial and difficult postings. But how much flexibility was really called for in serving as the Public Affairs Officer? Much of the job required standard, bureaucratic acumen. Each place had its USIS library to oversee with the same cloned collection of books, video tapes, and university catalogs. Each place had its cluster of local intellectuals and opinionated politicos to cultivate, who were always ready to either attend or address various artificial gatherings. Sure, Andrew made a point of balancing his guest lists with people from the local array of constituencies, but he usually got his pointers from other officers in the embassy, who saw to it that any real opposition to the local despot went uninvited. Maybe his problem was that he was too flexible.

Cheryl could trace Andrew's flexibility back to Peace Corps days in Liberia, where she had met him. They had both come to that adventure filled with the fervent naïveté of the times, ready to live side by side with natives in their villages, teaching children with grateful, beaming smiles in shadowy, mud-walled classrooms. Cheryl, fresh from marches down South, felt she'd achieved a kind of understanding, an actual form of integration with the Africans in a way that she'd found impossible back home. This didn't last long, of course, with a few bouts of malaria and dysentery, some untoward passes from the Liberian headmaster, and the ever more brazen pranks of her students. But it had stayed with her enough so that now, watching Mandy bully Faduma, she could feel a genuine twinge of embarrassment. She had to laugh at that young self, so earnestly mouthing the words to sappy folk songs at the party of Peace Corps volunteers where she had met Andrew. Where had all those "flowers" gone, anyway? Some went to USAID, others to State and USIS, a few cynics went straight to the CIA. All nomads except for the smart ones, who went home.

She had met Andrew near the end of her stay, in the compound of the Peace Corps Director in Monrovia. After a barbecue, after singing those songs under kerosene lanterns, she'd joined a group to go dancing at one of the flashier African bars. Andrew, who'd pulled faces at the folk music, danced with her persistently. She hadn't known what to make of the scrawny kid in his purple dashiki. He joked around with the musicians using the coastal pidgin and they laughed with him as if they were old friends. He knew the dance steps. Most of the volunteers relied on their versions of the boogaloo or the twist. His face was pale from too many bouts with malaria and covered in a clammy film of sweat—the kind of sweat they had all grown used to in that humid climate sans air conditioning. His paleness showed against his puffy red beard and the auburn hair that curled out wildly like Dylan's. For all his manic energy, she caught a sad look, a lonely one, in his pale blue eyes.

She went home with him that night to his mosquitoey mud house on the edge of town, with its citified tin roof. They talked and talked their hearts out. Then, before they made love, he raised the ante by rolling a joint. They smoked half of it and had sweet, sweaty, itchy sex. Afterward, he lit it again and, using a child's bubble blower he'd found in the market, they filled swirly bubbles with smoke, sending them high against the tin ceiling to confound the mosquitoes up there.

Maybe it was the excesses of those Peace Corps days, reported dutifully in some security file, that had held them back all these years. But that hardly seemed possible, since many of their friends had gone on up the ladder, people crazier than themselves. Such stuff was almost expected from those days. But in the Foreign Service, you could never know whether some rival might have planted a few defamatory seeds that could crop up later to tangle your way.

Cheryl took a tingling sip of her drink and blinked to be sure of what she was seeing. A bubble drifted along the balcony wall at eye level. It spun before her nose on an updraft and burst, leaving an ever so fine misting of Tide.

After supper, Cheryl took Mandy up to her room to read her a story. This was always a difficult time with Mandy. She knew Cheryl would be leaving her with Faduma for the evening, so she would balk at the cozy drowsiness Cheryl tried to lull into her. Cheryl just wished she'd fall asleep in her arms as she used to do. Nowadays she seemed spiteful in this wakefulness, as if she knew it hurt her mother that Faduma would be the one to finally tuck her in.

They were barely into the story when Mandy interrupted, "Can I watch the Smurfs tonight, Mommy, after the story? Please?"

"You've already seen enough video, sweetie. You need your sleep, you know."

"But Sesame's only a half hour."

Mandy began an awkward squirm in Cheryl's lap, shifting her weight so low that Cheryl had to pull her back up. Cheryl read on with firmness and Mandy dangled her weight slowly, subversively, all over again.

Andrew popped his head in the door. "The Husseins are here! Hurry, honey."

"Shoot!" she said. "You'd think these people would know to come late."

"They love these movies. Hey, listen to my intro: For the camel herding cowboys of the Ogaden, we present an American film classic about our nomads of the Wild West—*High Noon*!"

Mandy moaned, "Why can't I see the movie?"

"It's bedtime, baby. Andrew, would you call Faduma?"

Andrew's grin hung in thin air. He could grin like that for hours.

Mandy wouldn't have any more of Cheryl's lap. She wriggled down to the floor and went for her Cabbage Patch doll propped up on the pillows of her bed.

"We want to see the Smurfs, don't we, My Anne? Have to see the Smurfs."

The potato-faced doll beamed back a wide-eyed, accommodating grin.

When Faduma finally got to the room, Cheryl relented and told them to go watch the Smurfs.

As she walked down the front steps, she saw that the Husseins were already over by the bar. Andrew was at his post, greeting the British Ambassador at the gate. "So nice to see you!" she rehearsed, working her face into the evening's smile. She would go over and greet the Athertons and lead them down to meet the Husseins.

Andrew was busy talking up the wreck with Cyril Atherton, some rumor of a salvage ship unwilling to come down from the Gulf until insurance payments or the Somali government would cover costs.

Cheryl coaxed Grace Atherton to come with her down to the bar.

"I hope they get help soon," she said to Grace. "They need to keep those kids from swimming out to the sharks."

"Dreadful, really," Grace said. Her eyes drifted to a passing bubble. Then she added, "It's so kind of you to include us this evening. I just adore Gary Cooper."

"So do I," Cheryl said as they reached the couple at the bar. "You know the Husseins, don't you?"

"Indeed I do," Grace said, in her well-modulated English, leaving a note of irony for Cheryl to hear and the Husseins to miss. Abdulkadir Hussein was in charge of internal security, a job he was known to relish. "What a lovely dress, Mrs. Hussein."

"Thank you, Mrs. Atherton. I got it in Milan."

"Goodness, must have cost you a fortune."

Mrs. Hussein offered Grace the fabric on her sleeve to be touched appreciatively.

"Now tell me, Abdi," Grace started in, with friendly overfamiliarity. "How did the body of General Ali end up on the Lido beach, one thousand kilometers from Hargeisa?"

Cheryl winced inwardly at the bluntness of Grace's questioning, even while noticing that Abdi didn't bat an eye.

"Ah, Mrs. Atherton, the secessionists have plenty of means to bring him down from the North. This act is a silly threat which will get them nowhere."

"Indeed, it would seem a gesture completely out of service to their own interests, don't you think? Inviting harsh reprisals from the government."

"Yes, the secessionists do seem to be inviting discipline."

"But tell me, Abdi. Precisely how would they transport the body fresh without an airplane?"

"Well, Mrs. Atherton, perhaps they kidnapped him and spirited him over the border with the assistance of their Ethiopian allies. Once they reached the South, it would take but a day to drive him into town and execute him on the beach."

"Quite. But I understand he was seen in Hargeisa just last Thursday. Hardly time for such an expedition."

Cheryl admired the pluck Grace showed in her questions, playing half the old colonial matron, half the human rights advocate.

"Madame, we have already sent a diplomatic note to Addis. I must say, you British seem to always give the North more credit than they are due."

"Surely you don't believe I've declared for the secessionists, Abdi? Tell me, now. What have you done to keep the kids from swimming out to the damned old wreck?"

Grace kept up her little inquisition with the Husseins as Cheryl took her leave to greet newly arriving guests.

These were the moments Cheryl hated, introductions among the meagre beginnings of the guest list and starting up little conversations. It usually didn't last long but, this night, with the bubbles coming in lightly, intermittently, quietly threatening a blizzard, time passed much too slowly. Finally, she had groups of guests spun together in small circles, drinks in hand, and Andrew joined the party, leaving the latecomers to find their way to the patio.

Talk was full of the ship: the nature of the bubbles, rumors of toxic cargoes left off the ship's manifest—Israeli goods en route to South Africa, the danger of the ship eventually breaking up as it was forced further aground, the need for a salvage ship that might never come, should the rumor about Liberian insurance prove true. And the situation in the North being the underlying reason, whispered by the diplomats when amongst themselves, why the government was unwilling to divert funds for the salvage efforts. Rumors usually nourished the dull parties in

Mog, but with bubbles beginning to fly willy-nilly, Cheryl worried her party would spin well beyond control.

She saw the Rosens finally arrive. Ruth Rosen was always so practical about these affairs. She treated everything as part of the job. After greetings, Dave lit up a cigar and joined the circle of military attachés. Cheryl took Ruth aside.

"What am I going to do about these bubbles?"

"Nothing, naturally," Ruth said in her confident deadpan.

"But everybody is worried about the rumors of poison. If it gets any worse, they'll want to go in the house."

"Baloney. It's just laundry detergent. Dave had it checked out. Ship's manifest has twenty tons of Tide destined for Mombasa."

"Ha!"

"So relax, the party looks great. Come on, let's mingle."

They were waiting now for General Mahmoud. Cheryl watched Andrew across the patio. He was swatting bubbles, laughing in a group with Dave Rosen and the DCM, probably joking away mosquitoes along with any rumors of further terrorist activity seeping in from the North. There was a time when Andrew would have mocked himself, chided himself, for cozying up to the military types and their fervent support for the dictatorship. He would have laughed at their simple belief that the right amount of money and arms could actually buy them geopolitical ascendancy on the Horn of Africa. Andrew now saved his irony for lighter topics.

Finally, the general arrived with the rumbling of his

motorcycle escort outside the gate. Andrew dropped his floating State Department smile and gathered his seriousness to meet him. After a decent interval for a last drink and a little chit chat with the general, Cheryl gracefully directed the guests toward their seats.

Andrew blew his introduction, leaving out camels and nomads and the Ogaden. "Somalia is not the only country to have cowboys," he said. But he got the group to laugh through the introduction anyway, punctuating the last sentence with a pistol gesture of his thumb and index finger popping an approaching bubble.

Cheryl turned off the patio lights and slipped away from the flickering wall. She went in to check on Mandy, who was sound asleep on Faduma's lap, the blue light of the Smurfs notwithstanding.

By morning, the blizzard had passed. The drifts along the seawall had melted down to dusty, sooty traces, like old snow. The ship hulked a little closer to shore, though the low tide made it seem closer still. A crack showed itself near the middle of the high deck.

"Looks like it'll break any time now," Andrew said. "Maybe this will get them motivated about a salvage contract."

"I doubt it," Cheryl said. General Mahmoud had been noncommittal on the subject at the party. She reached over and touched Andrew's arm. "Don't slow down. We've got to get to school."

The huge rocking thing made her dizzy just to look at it. This daily contemplation of the wreck was beginning to wear thin.

At school, Cheryl's second graders were antsy. All they wanted to do was talk about the ship. She was midway through their spelling test when, through the open door, she saw the gunny sergeant jump out of the embassy van in full battle regalia.

"He's acting like we're facing a coup d'etat!" she thought. Normally he wore one of those Marine Happy Hour t-shirts emblazoned with a camel and the line, "Sunny Mogadishu - A vacation spot like no other." He marched into Chris Walinski's office at the head of the covered walkway.

"F-E-L-L-O-W," she continued with the spelling test. "He is a fine fellow. F-E-L-L-O-W."

She kept an eye on the principal's door and waited for the children to write down the word. It took three more words from her spelling list before the gunny sergeant strode out of the office. Chris stood stolidly at the door and waved him a civilian's salute. The van churned dust out the drive and disappeared behind a row of stunted frangipanis.

Chris took too many minutes, too many more words down the list, to leave his office and spread the news. Whenever he had to call a special meeting, he made it a practice to announce it personally. She studied his face as he marched past the climbing jasmine that trimmed the front walkway. As usual, his expression remained irritatingly impassive. First, he entered the teacher's lounge. Then, at last, he took the walkway toward her room.

"Children, turn your papers over. I have to talk to Mr. Walkinski. Nils, that means you!"

She stepped outside the door. "What's up Chris?"

"It's just the ship," he said, in his best bored voice. "It has caught fire. There's some smoke, and they're going to close up the embassy. We're advised that the school is perfectly safe."

"Safe! What about Andrew? The people in the embassy?"

"They'll stay inside for the moment." Chris pressed on with his announcement. "The wind is blowing the stuff northwest. We're in the safest spot in town."

"Wait a minute, Chris. Blowing what stuff?"

"Well, we don't really know. The ship is beginning to split up and in the process one of the containers inside got twisted until the chemicals in it ignited. There's some other stuff on fire from it."

"Jesus!"

"Listen Cheryl, we need to keep the kids calm. It may be that we'll have to keep them here a little longer today. I'll let everybody know as soon as I get more word over the radio net."

He turned and strolled on down to the next classroom.

Cheryl couldn't trust Chris any more than she could trust Andrew. These men treated everyone as a security risk, Chris using his dull officiousness and Andrew using his humor. Why keep secrets? In the interest of pedagogical security? Chris was hiding something. Surely, he knew which "stuff" was burning, specifically. She would follow his orders, giving the kids a quiet assignment, and giving herself more time to think. She passed out subtraction table worksheets.

It galled her that she was expected to adjust to this damn post without adequate knowledge of the whole situation. There was an unwritten code she had to follow in playing a diplomat's wife. She was to look as assured and confident as her husband, but she was to have none of the inside story. Like Ruth Rosen, she must aspire to become a PEW: Perfect Embassy Wife. She felt more like a Prisoner of Embassy Wisdom at the moment. In the most serious things, Andrew always kept mum. In past crises, like the civil war in the North and the hostages held there, she'd had to gather most of her information from rumors in the teacher's lounge—rumors Andrew would encourage her to share with him, even as he carefully divulged well edited, but supposedly sincere, shared facts. It was all a game to him, but now he was in danger, and she was expected to act normally.

The kids in third grade were shouting out of turn for some game, probably Sunita's version of Hangman. Sunita hadn't learned the rules of it yet, let alone basic classroom management. So much for keeping the school quiet. Cheryl's kids were rushing through their worksheets, racing for the chance to talk again.

Mrs. Caputo came to the door, eyebrows furrowed in worry. Her lower lip slid nervously over her upper lip as if she had just stopped talking to herself.

"Madame Brown," she said in a whisper, "I've come to take Manuela with me." She waited until Cheryl got out the door and then she wheezed, "Oh, isn't it terrible?"

"What's terrible?"

"The ship. It's going to explode! We go to Afgooye. Our ambassador is telling all Italians to go out to Afgooye. Manuela, my dear, come."

Mrs. Caputo drew her daughter down the walkway in a shoulder hold, kissing her forehead, breathing anxieties into her ear.

"Be quiet!" Cheryl said firmly to the class. "Get back to work."

"But Mrs. Brown, the ship?" Janice Rosen pleaded. "Manuela's mother said the ship?"

"Never mind Manuela's mother."

She wanted to comfort the class, to quiet them gracefully. It embarrassed her sense of professionalism when she fell into snappy commands, but she didn't have the patience to do anything better. She would let Ruth, in fourth grade, comfort her daughter at break. The spelling tests needed to be corrected. She sat down at her desk and just looked at the papers. Afgooye, the little plantation town, lay twenty miles inland to the south, behind the coastal dunes in a little river valley. She realized her heart was palpitating, and it had been at it for some time now, speeding up until she had to notice it: The hell with Afgooye, give me the Nairobi Hilton!

"No," she stopped herself, half with humor, though her heart kept racing, "Beam me up, Scotty. Beam me outta here and set me down in Falls Church." This didn't help. Below her heart, her stomach felt hollow, tightening in a knot around nothing, a squishy knot that might loosen in a moment. Cars were pulling into the parking lot; more kids were leaving. Her class was working itself into a low-grade hum.

She stood up and passed back the spelling tests. If they corrected them all together, one kid at a time coming to the board to spell out each word, she might focus them until break. She closed the door to keep their eyes off the parking lot.

At the bell, the kids surged down the walkway to the playground that faced the city.

Ruth came to her room from the back terrace, "You've gotta see this, Cheryl!"

She pointed over the playground filled with spellbound children, out past the sand dunes to a roiling black column that leaned over the city. She gave Janice, who was holding her by the waist, a quick hug around the shoulders. Then she urged her out to the playground to join the kids who were beginning to play. Cheryl pulled Ruth into the empty classroom.

"We've got to do something," Ruth said in a rush. "Mrs. Mueller says her embassy is evacuating their houses in the Lido, downwind from it. Toxic. It's very toxic. If a certain container hits seawater it'll set off an explosion, a toxic explosion worse than Bhopal. They're talking a two- to three-mile radius. And anywhere up to a hundred miles downwind. It could kill two hundred thousand downtown and along the Lido alone."

"Oh God! And what about the smoke?"

"Who the hell knows what that is? All I know is, Chris has to do something about this!"

They rushed toward his office, but Mrs. Hussein stopped them on the way.

"I must find my children!"

"Check the playground. But wait, please tell us what's happening."

"You must know. You Americans know everything."

"We hear about chemicals."

"Not chemicals. Ten times worse! The Israelis, you know, the Israelis are secretly shipping atomic materials, they call 'fashionable materials,' to South Africa. A fireball up to ten kilometers wide! My God, you imagine!"

Mrs. Hussein hurried down the walkway, the powder blue gauze of her shawl fluttering at her elbow.

"A fireball?" Cheryl frowned. "That's hardly possible. You have to have an actual bomb to get that."

But still, in Cheryl's imagination, a huge dome, translucent, rose over the city: one of those sci-fi crystal hemispheres meant to protect a space colony, except it clouded inside, frosting up like the fuzzy first pulse of an atomic explosion, filling it to bursting with a whomp, then following massively into a mushroom cloud.

"No matter what it is," Ruth said, "we've got to get our kids out of here."

Cheryl liked Ruth's take-charge attitude. She knew how to handle a post like Mog. She'd been through the trouble in Islamabad and other places. She knew what to do.

As they entered the office, Ruth barked her question, "Chris, just exactly what is going on?"

He frowned up from his messy desk, trying to look annoyed at the interruption.

"The situation is under control," he said calmly.

Cheryl pressed him, "How can you sit there and say

something like that? Parents are picking up kids right and left. And Mrs. Caputo…"

"Mrs. Caputo, if you don't mind my saying so, is a little crazy. I called the Italian Embassy and they are not, I repeat *not,* evacuating their people."

Ruth jumped in, "The Germans are."

"Listen," he said. "Your responsibility is to your students. The best way to help them is to keep calm yourselves."

"Right, keep them calm instead of evacuating them right now."

Cheryl pleaded, "Chris you've got to tell us more."

"I don't know anymore."

"Alright, be that way. I'll call Andrew on the radio myself," Cheryl sputtered.

She pulled the microphone loose from the lunchbox radio on his desk.

"Eagle's Nest, Eagle's Nest. This is Eagle 42."

The voice of the duty Marine droned in, "This is Eagle's Nest."

"Give me Eagle 42. You know who. The other one."

The radio blew static. Then, "Eagle 42b, 42a is in a meeting. Nest out."

"Country Team meeting," Cheryl said. "They'd better be planning a full-scale evacuation!" She caught her voice cracking. "I just knew it was bad."

Ruth squeezed her elbow in support.

"Chris, we can't wait for them to decide," Ruth said. "Look, we've got at least eight vehicles here. We can drive all the kids that are left out to Afgooye."

"They can fly a plane in from Nairobi," Cheryl joined in. "Land right out on the highway."

"At least we'll be safe, Chris," Ruth went on. "We can't wait for the Country Team. They've probably locked themselves into the safe room down there and they won't leave until the smoke clears. They just haven't thought it all out yet, Chris."

Cheryl could picture Andrew and Dave huddled down in that shielded communications room with the DCM and the rest, mumbling at each other through gas masks.

"Ruth. Cheryl. You're exaggerating things. Go and attend to your classes. Please! Calm down."

He glared at them as if he took them about as seriously as Lucy and Ethel. They backed out of the office, Ruth muttering something about bringing this up at the next school board meeting, if they'd ever have one.

Cheryl's class was down to five students after break. It would have been down to four, but Ruth convinced Janice to stay with her proper room, just as Mandy was still staying with the kindergartners. Cheryl was glad the kindergartners had their separate little playground, where the building hid the view of the black column. Mandy seemed just fine there, for the time being. Cheryl's students were wild about the smoke. She explained to them it was just like the smoke from burning rubber they sometimes saw coming out of the city dump. Even though the breeze that came in through the louvered glass windows blew clean and straight off the Indian Ocean, she found herself irritated by it, worried it would somehow veer off its steady monsoonal course.

With so few students left, she let them group around a couple of board games. She sat down to look at the stories they'd written the day before. Three of them were illustrated at the top half of the page with crayon renditions of the boat, their awkward lines matching the wobbly look of the wreck. All they needed was smoke. What if Andrew and Dave really were trapped? She couldn't help but worry. Andrew would be cracking jokes to keep their spirits up as they planned the evacuation and called in a plane through the embassy in Nairobi. But he would be serious, too. Serious for Mandy's sake, and Cheryl's. She couldn't remember ever seeing gas masks or oxygen bottles in the embassy. So much for being on the Country Team. So much for being second in line to the DCM when the ambassador was out of town. What good would that do if they were all turning blue down there, choking, gagging, spitting up blood? She couldn't stand it. Get us out, Andrew, please get us out! Cheryl stood up to busy herself out of her fears and hovered over the kids at their games. It was nearly an hour before she saw Chris start on his rounds again. She met him at the door.

"The embassy has given us the all clear. The fire has died down," he declared.

"Whew!"

"We'll let school out as usual, but buses will take the outer road around town for the kids on the Lido side. You'll need to ride with them because Andrew called to say he won't be able to get across town."

"Then it's not all clear."

"Well, there is some concern now about civil unrest downtown. People still panicking to get out. At least the smoke is not a problem anymore."

He moved on to the next classroom, carrying his tight little ass like a Sunday School superintendent.

The bus ride home was awful. All the kids were wild because of the detour. They wouldn't obey the Somali bus driver nor the young Danish mother who served as a monitor. Cheryl sat near the front with Mandy and tried to ignore the racket; she could think of nothing she could do that would help the monitor. She stared out the window as the bus made its way up the dune hills on the outer periphery of the city, past slopes dotted with squatters' dwellings. The little gnomic domes were patched with pink and white and blue plastic shopping bags, ragged black plastic sheeting, and pieces of cardboard. In form they were perfect, just like the traditional nomad domed huts, but they lacked the wonderful fiber mats that the women wove out in the desert. These nomads had escaped grim famines and clan wars to come here, where they could forage little better than the cattle along the roadside that chewed dry sticks and newspapers. Of all days to have to look at this, along with the parade of donkey carts slowing traffic. Those mangy donkeys sickened her, pulling their flimsy carts that rolled along on truck tires, each one sporting a stripe across the shoulder like a pennant from their zebra days. And she wanted no more of the herds of dusty camels either, scavenging a last feed before their march down to the sea for export to Arabia.

The bus reached a developed neighborhood with rows of tea houses, shops, and video stores plastered with posters of Indian and Italian movie stars. The streets were crowded, and the bus had to slow even more as it neared the hustle of the khat market. Surrounded by all this bustling and shouting, the children in the bus quieted down. Realizing the bus usually never took this road, Cheryl half expected a stone through the windshield. But there were other little yellow and green Toyota buses just like it, and it seemed to take a while for people to notice hers was filled with the children of foreigners. She was relieved when they finally reached the broad boulevard that circled back down toward the sea and her house.

She entered the house with a taste of revulsion that had been growing on the long drive. The smell inside the foyer only heightened it, turning her stomach. This was a smoky, chemical stench—the kind from botched experiments left too long on Bunsen burners in chemistry class. Faduma greeted her with an interoffice envelope brought by the embassy van driver. She fussed with the little string that wound around the plastic tab, wondering what Andrew had to say, and pulled out a yellow sheet of legal notepaper. He'd scrawled, "Pack for an overnight and a wake-up at the Rosens'. I'll be home soon. Waiting on a cable from DC." A wake-up? It was the phrase people used when their time at post was short. They'd count the days and tack on a wake-up for the day they were scheduled to fly out. He was secretly telling her they would be going to Nairobi after all. The Rosens lived on the safer side of town, near the airport. She wondered which it would be: a C-130 or a chartered commercial jet? With her luck it would be a C-130, but at least they were getting out of this place!

"Mandy, I want you to go with Faduma and take a nice bath. I have to pack. We're going to the Rosens' tonight, and real early tomorrow morning we're flying to Nairobi."

"Oh goodie!" she cheered, hardly knowing where Nairobi was. "But, can I watch Sesame?"

"Maybe, after your bath. We'll see when Daddy gets here."

Cheryl packed the important articles in Andrew's carry-on satchel: the little Sony shortwave for news, the credit cards that were useless in Mog, traveler's checks, black diplomatic passports, and the blue ones they were supposed to switch to in the event of a hijacking. Then she picked out some nice outfits to wear around the Hilton and warm clothes—jackets and sweaters—for those cool Nairobi nights. In Andrew's garment bag she loaded up dress shirts and slacks, his blue suit, and his woolly tweed jacket that smelled a little sour for lack of wear. Tomorrow night they'd be dining at the Amboseli Grill, planning out their itinerary. Andrew might have to stay a few weeks in Nairobi to wait things out, perhaps even return to Mog after things cleared up. But she could certainly head back to their house in Falls Church.

When she was finished, she had Abdullah carry the luggage down to the foyer, and she took a long hot shower. As she was drying off, she heard Andrew honk at the gate for the guard. She heard Mandy calling to him, "Nairobi! Nairobi!" echoing through the house and then his steps, heavy with Mandy on his hip, climbing to the upper level.

"What's this Nairobi business?" he shouted through the steam in the bathroom. It was too foggy to make out his face, but the tone was angry and sarcastic at once.

"You said an overnight and a wake-up."

Steam whirled around the split figure, Mandy still at his hip. The room cleared as it wafted out the door. She could see his face now, dropping his scowl for a stern, somewhat long-suffering expression of pity.

"I'm sorry if you took it that way. I just wanted you to pack for an overnighter. I wanted you to know we'd be back home soon, no later than tomorrow night."

She felt like crying but anger surfaced to counter it.

"You mean to tell me it's not safe enough to stay here tonight, but it's not dangerous enough to get out of this stinking, poisoned town! How can the Rosens' be any safer?"

"They're over by the school," he said matter-of-factly.

"So, toxins are still blowing off the ship, right? And we're probably steeped in carcinogens this very minute."

"No, no, no, honey! It's just a precaution. There's an EPA team flying in from DC. In a couple of days, we'll have a clear picture."

"Then it's really a longer stay at the Rosens'. Good thing I packed plenty of clothes, though they might just get a little sweaty for Mog. Meanwhile, our lungs are about to collapse."

"That's all over, Cheryl, really. The only real concern

now is about some heavy metals. Some kind of mercury. Could eventually contaminate the harbor. No more lobster, that's all. Unless, of course, people might be tempted by Day-Glo red lobsters," he said, flashing a winning smile at her.

"Aren't you mixing that up with the Israeli plutonium?"

He snickered. Just like him, the silly bastard.

"You heard that one, too?" he said, barely holding back his laughter. "Nothing to it."

"No shit! Well it had some of us up in the air, like about ten miles up. Andrew, what the fuck? … Oh, Jesus!" She stopped herself and called out, "Faduma, would you come take Mandy for a minute?"

They stared at each other, Mandy rubbing tears into My Anne's yarn dreadlocks, until Faduma came and carried her away.

"Andrew, why didn't you call me?"

"I was busy with the emergency."

"I even tried to reach you on the radio."

"Oh, come on, hon. I'm sorry. There was just so much to do."

He placed his hands on her shoulders and playfully straightened them. She shook them off and walked into the bedroom.

"Have it your way," she said, as she put away the khaki safari outfit she'd set aside for the trip and grabbed a cotton sundress.

They took to the outer road at dusk. Andrew drove carefully through the traffic and milling crowds. Cheryl let herself imagine it was their last drive across town, closing her eyes to the donkey carts and the silhouettes of long-necked camels craning down at her. The car engine's drone took on the comforting hum of a 747.

Ruth fixed sloppy joes for the bunch. Cheryl liked that. Ruth wasn't one to stand on ceremony. She made something easy for the crowd. Nobody was hungry except the kids, anyway. And after supper, she took the kids in tow.

"Tommy, Janice, Mandy," she bellowed good-naturedly, "I've got a new video from home. Starts with *Family Ties*."

The kids all screamed a chorus of, "Yippee," and flopped down in front of the set. Mandy cradled My Anne, half strangling the thing to get her thumb around to her mouth. Then Ruth wheeled out a cart of liqueurs and joined the adults at the table. Cheryl took a Drambuie, while Andrew and Dave went for snifters of cognac. Ruth poured herself a sherry.

"A fine way to cleanse the palate," Andrew said, raising his snifter appreciatively.

"Are you casting aspersions on my cooking?" Ruth asked tartly.

"Not at all, Ruth, darling. It's just that I thought I'd never get my taste buds to work again what with all that awful smoke this afternoon."

Dave grunted his assent and took out a cigar. He snipped off the tip with his fancy brass clipper and lit it up. "It was pretty rich down there," he commented, leaning back in his chair to blow his smoke off to the corner.

Cheryl couldn't believe Dave would actually light up the cigar amid all this talk of the smoke, but that was just like him. He was as unconscious of his self-absorbed actions as Andrew. Or, worse yet, he was willfully engaging in his habit because he really didn't care about the alarming events of the day.

"How about a little bridge?" Ruth suggested. "That ought to clear our heads."

"Sure, why not?" Cheryl answered.

Dave slid down a notch in his chair—a move like bored compliance—and waited for Ruth to get the cards.

They played into a half-hearted game, Andrew always overextending Cheryl's closely factored hands. They all were drinking more than they should, although Andrew seemed to let it affect him the most. He was dredging up old jokes and stories Cheryl had almost forgotten and wished she had. Finally, she had to tell him to pay attention.

"But I am," he snapped.

"No, you're not. You're not keeping track of the game. You're not listening to my cues."

"You're just not catching my signals," he bluffed back, winking with clownish exaggeration.

Everyone but Cheryl chuckled. Ruth took a moment, with all cards face down, to top off their drinks.

"Ruth," Cheryl asked, "Dave didn't happen to send you any signals today, did he?""Oh, come on Cheryl," Andrew chided.

"I'll bet he didn't even send you a note like my gallant, if ever so uninformative, Galahad sent me."

Everyone was quiet then except for the gentle lisp of Dave drawing on his cigar.

"Hell, he told me to get ready for an overnight and a wake-up! You know," Cheryl dug in sharply, "like we're heading out to Nairobi. At least Dave doesn't subject you to that kind of stuff, does he Ruth?"

Andrew was slowly hunching his shoulders, gathering his hands around the snifter in his lap. His smoothly shaven cheeks were reddening, flushed at the thought of the effect of Cheryl's behavior on his next performance review.

"Cheryl," Ruth started, leaning her elbows forward on the table and slowly twisting the stem of her sherry glass, "We've all had a rough day. Things are better now. Really."

"You weren't saying that this afternoon," Cheryl said, trying to keep her voice below the video. "You were second-guessing the guys just like I was. We almost caravanned the kids out to Afgooye, you know," she said, turning to Dave. "Would have been pretty funny, huh? You would have liked that, wouldn't you Dave? Andrew? The DCM would have been proud of your wives. Shit, he'd be sure to ask the ambassador to give us a commendation for bravery, eh? Just count on a bevy of PEWs to save the day!"

"Oh, come on honey, stop it!" Andrew reached for his hand of cards, taking a quick peak, trying to edge her back into the game.

"Don't you want to know, Ruth? Don't you want to know if they actually ever even thought of evacuating us?"

Ruth looked over at Dave, who was now glowering under a cloud of smoke. She seemed to be gathering her courage, ready to face him as she had faced Chris at school.

"Come on, let's get real about this. No secrets here. Not this time, goddammit. Ask him, Ruth."

"Well, Dave?" Ruth started in, and Cheryl was glad she'd finally joined her.

"It crossed our minds," Dave said with a voice that sifted gravel.

"What kept you from it?" Ruth pressed.

Cheryl was fascinated by the look on Andrew's face as he watched Dave. His mouth had actually dropped open.

"DCM wouldn't buy it. Not with the ambassador out of town. Not without more information," Dave answered.

"So you cabled DC for those EPA types," Cheryl said.

Andrew jumped in, "That was more to help the Somalis, should there be any danger of the harbor getting polluted."

"Bullshit! You mean, that's the excuse you're going to use when the ambassador gets back," Cheryl said triumphantly. "But behind it all was your chickenshit unwillingness to bite the damn bullet and evacuate us in the face of danger."

Both men sat silent. Cheryl looked over to Ruth and said, "That pretty much clears it up for me. You interested in finding out if these guys are willing to cough up a couple of tickets, say, for tomorrow's Kenya Airways flight? We could clean out our kids' lungs in one of those lodges up the slope of Mount Kenya."

This stopped Andrew, mid pour another finger of

cognac. He looked across the table at her with worried wonder.

"Let's be rational about this," Dave said, his voice taking on its deep, sonorous authority. "Of course, we were all scared, it's only natural. But, really, we do have a pretty good idea of what's on the ship now, thanks to the Germans. They were the ones who started the crazy rumors. I called the German attaché myself this afternoon, and we got together with the ship's captain down in the jail. Went over the ship's manifest with a fine-tooth comb this time. Everything checks out clean. Nothing toxic. Nothing that would be explosive and toxic, anyway. Just those shipments of mercuric whatever, and that stuff will just sink, roll around on the bottom where a salvage ship can easily suck it up. I'm satisfied that we're all pretty safe, Cheryl. I'd like you to believe me. Really, everything is going to be okay."

Andrew breathed out noisily and took a sip of his cognac. Cheryl began to feel a little embarrassed, as if she'd just gotten over an adolescent tiff with her father. Maybe Dave was satisfied, and Ruth along with him, but things didn't sound at all steady yet to her. She took up Andrew's gesture though—his stiff, quick nod of ass-kissing acquiescence—to put an end to the awkwardness. Then she looked over into the living room where *Cheers* had begun playing, generating hilarity out of its studio audience, though the kids sat quietly puzzling at jokes that went over their heads. Mandy lay sound asleep on the rug with My Anne tucked under her chin.

"I appreciate your candor, Dave," she said, as she got up. "Excuse me while I put Mandy to bed."

She stooped down a little dizzily to pick up Mandy and stowed My Anne on Mandy's chest. Then she stood up slowly, steadying herself so the others wouldn't have to worry about her carrying Mandy up the stairs. She worked her way up the tile stairs and down the bend of the hallway into the guest room, which was positively cold. The light from the hallway shone on a large mattress on the floor that was neatly made up for Mandy. A king-sized bed stood next to it in the shadows, just beneath the air conditioner. Against the far wall were stacks of canned soda pop, along with cases of wine and beer, cartons of Fritos, Planters peanuts, marshmallows, and such. It was obvious the Rosens kept this room cold at all times; it was their special storeroom for consumables from the States. The extra luxury of around the clock air-conditioning in the Third World preserved precious perishables like taco shells, freeing them of the taste of cardboard, so that the Rosens could close their shades on any given night and imagine they were back home. Cheryl pulled back the covers and put Mandy down, gently straightening her pjs to cover her arms and legs and settling My Anne down beside her. She drew the covers up to Mandy's chin and tucked them firmly under the mattress.

Stepping unsteadily onto the bed, she reached up and turned off the air conditioner. She would let the room warm up a little, then she'd turn it on low. She could wait to do that. No need to go back to the table after what she'd said. Exhaustion drew her down and she sat on the side of the bed, staring out at the streetlights and the distant sprinkling of lights across the city. She felt a little sickened by the woozy, loose action of the bed springs.

It was all quite simple, really. Andrew had betrayed them. He'd kept his eye on his career, on the excitement of the Country Team meeting and the sense of power he gathered there, completely oblivious to the smoke outside, to the poison and danger that Mandy and Cheryl faced by staying here with him. While the ship rocked and swayed its loose and tumbling cargo—beached, burning, and billowing for all to see—he'd joked and acquiesced. He'd dutifully sent out cables, complete with bureaucratic niceties, through the proper channels, managing the crisis with his polished efficiency and, no doubt, with a certain pride in a job well done. Then he'd scribbled out his careless note to her, taking her trust and loyalty for granted. He'd been operating like this for years, from post to post, and it was only now she could clearly see it. That coup in Guinea should have clued her in, when she had spent the first night scared and alone while he stayed at the embassy helping to monitor the situation, as he put it. That was a heady adventure—nerve-wracking, yet also exciting—but it was before Mandy was born, and the frightening parts had gradually faded in the incessant moves to new posts. Now Andrew's game embarrassed her with its obviousness. It had been right there in front of her eyes, and she'd been unwilling to see it looming, huge, as ugly and hulking as the grounded freighter lolling in the harbor.

She had to laugh at her blindness to this blatant image of their marriage—this marriage on the rocks. She'd come all this way to find it, but not until she'd had to stare daily at this rocking, smoking, bubbling mess. Just how much had she closed herself, numbed herself, to Andrew's silliness, to his desperate, ambitious foolishness? It had only seemed to register to her as a mild irritant, hardly noticed, like the buzzing of locusts in the thorn trees. Now, in her embarrassment at having been played the hysterical fool, the irritation shuddered into honest revulsion.

The solution was easy—simple as TV, smooth as a soap opera. She could leave and take Mandy with her, start up her own life where she'd left off in Georgetown. She could stay in their house in Falls Church for the time being. She might need more money than she could get in a no-fault divorce, but there was mental cruelty, even physical endangerment. She could use these kinds of arguments to get a decent settlement, couldn't she? It had been so long since she'd spent time back home, there were bound to be lots of new ways to work it out. She would start by demanding that airplane ticket home.

Andrew's silhouette gathered at the door. He tiptoed in, carefully skirting Mandy's mattress, and sat down beside Cheryl, setting the bed springs to rocking. His arm settled its sweaty warmth around her shoulders, drawing her in, his hot breath rank with cognac and the piercing redolence of cigars. She shuddered in his cloying hold and shook her shoulders free so she could stand and turn on the air conditioner.

"It's over, Andrew. I'm sorry, but it's over." She did not sit back down.

"Aw, come on! You're joking," he said, his voice loud, incredulous.

"Quiet. Your daughter is asleep. She needs the rest for the flight to Nairobi tomorrow."

"Honey. No." He whispered.

She did not reply.

"Please give me a chance. Not like this, hon. Please!"

He couldn't come up with lines any better than those out of his classic B movies. It was easy for her to feed him back in kind.

"Why not like this?" she hissed, keeping her voice barely audible over the hum of the air conditioner. "Too messy for your career?"

"No, that's not true."

"You don't even care what's true anymore, Andrew. It *would* be messy! A good PEW never leaves post in a huff. You don't have to lie to placate me. Surely you can be honest enough to admit you care about your career, whether you care about me or not."

"But I do care about you."

"See? You're hopeless. You don't get it."

"Hon, you're being unfair. I love you. I love Mandy. There is no way I could stand to lose you. Maybe I haven't been showing it like I should."

"That's because you can't. You're like a locust. A hard shell has crept over your tenderness. You just buzz with easy lines and silly jokes, deadening all feeling around you. You're not the Andrew I knew and loved back in Monrovia. He would have been the first to blow a raspberry in the DCM's face."

"I'll change. Please give me the chance."

"You changed a long time ago. It's just taken me awhile to see it."

Cheryl lay down next to Mandy on the mattress, cuddling close to her under the covers. She heard the bed creak as it swayed when Andrew flopped his back down on it. He let out a ragged sigh that turned into short, wrenching sobs.

His crying disgusted her even as it moved her to want to comfort him. Let him feel this, she thought. She would go to Nairobi with Mandy. Maybe stay a week to let it sink in. She might consider coming back if he really sounded like he cared over the phone. Next summer, during home leave, they might get some help to sort out whatever they were not able to resolve on their own.

But God help him if he should call her up and start in with a single pun.

Great Barrier Reef

I had already decided that if they told me it had metastasized to my lymph nodes I wouldn't try to go back to work. I wouldn't hang around for debilitating chemo and last-ditch surgeries either. I'd head for the Great Barrier Reef and scuba dive, while I still had my strength and could enjoy it. My passion for diving had been stoked along the Somali coast where I was working for a relief agency. If I was going to die, I felt I owed it to myself to see the Great Barrier Reef first. It wouldn't matter by then if my skin took on more exposure to the intense sun, because the cancer would already be working inside me. I didn't tell anybody my plan, because I knew it sounded selfish. To let anyone know I was even thinking about it showed I was already giving up.

I didn't want anyone to come with me. I would fly there by myself. I'd take a couple preliminary dives to really soak up the beauty of the reef—everything magnified in my face mask by the water, the thrill of currents playing through the soft fingers of sea anemones as clown fish hovered above them, the immediacy of being immersed in the welter of life there. Then I'd go down to a stretch I liked, some tide hollowed coral canyon, and glide out of it past the edge of the reef escarpment like a plane flying out of broken buttes and mesas into the blue, and down past the point of surfacing, down to where I would succumb to the rapture of the deep, and I would just kick deeper down, feeling the crazy rapture unto death.

In the lab they were slicing sections of my nodes—opaque squid flesh—and examining each piece. It took days as I waited around the hospital in Georgetown. They wanted to be sure. I did, too.

They gave me a reprieve. They told me I was lucky because it had been on my arm. Since nothing showed in the nodes of my armpit, they'd as good as cut it off at the pass. I went back to my work in Africa.

Activity around the warehouses of the old port was as busy and ineffectual as ever. My agency had been charged with the coordination of all relief supplies coming into the country, and the old port's warehouses had been put at our disposal for this purpose. Where the new port across the harbor radiated efficiency, huge cranes akimbo, ours was a ship's graveyard. The place was a rust heap of old tugs and vintage PT boats dry-docked since the Italians surrendered Mogadishu in WWII. There were even the scattered spines of a few ancient Arab dhows scavenged of most of their wood. When I first came to the country, I joined a couple of expats who were restoring a small Italian fishing boat that had been half-sunk in the sand. It seemed now like it was one of the few boats that had ever gotten out of that junkyard. I could hardly wait to go out fishing in it again as soon as work got sorted out, but I knew that might take a long time.

Part of my job was to see to it that trucks hauled our containers from the new port alongside the narrow streets of the old stone town, Hamar Weyne, over to our warehouses. It would have been easier to have ships unload directly onto our docks, but the planks had rotted, and our part of the harbor hadn't been dredged in decades. The new harbor was a boon to the country's donor economy. All sorts of ships could stop there now. But the big cut in the reef had also let in sharks. Kids playing soccer on the Lido beach lost legs and lives just chasing out after the ball. Nobody did anything about it, just like nobody did much about anything here.

I was back in the Third World and my job was to help prop it up. That's exactly how I phrased it to myself standing out on the splintered dock, and the cynicism of it didn't surprise me. I'd long since given up the idealism of my early volunteer days. As a maintenance and logistics officer, I now looked at things more practically. I had to make sure the agency's fleet of trucks continued rolling out to the refugee camps in the desert and that just about everything else kept running—like our office backup generator, which kept the computer people happy and air-conditioned, and even the plumbing in the agency rep's house, which kept his wife happy. I could contract out some of the work, but when I did, it seemed like I always had to have my own crew redo it. Haggling with Somali contractors was never a win-win proposition.

There I was with one more year to go on my

contract, and that first day back I wondered if I could stand it. Across the water, Hamar Weyne held no charm. Whitewashed stone buildings with domes and minarets couldn't hide its festering decrepitude. The harbor flats at low tide in the midday heat stank of it. Busy as ants, a pack of kids chased down the beach after yet another ball. My head mechanic was threatening to quit and go work for the oil prospectors, and my boss was insisting I come to his place for supper. I just wanted to be left alone to get used to the idea of being back, but it already seemed like I'd never been gone.

Geoff and Sandi Winter were full of the latest gossip and rumors. The civil war in the North was heating up. Our trucks had been stopped and ransacked by the army just south of Beled Weyne. The UN High Commissioner was lodging a formal protest, as were the usual embassies. There was talk of a coup and the duty-free shop was out of beer. Geoff was down to three cases of Heineken. I raised my glass to that. And, there was the latest affair—the same old shit. But something had changed. I looked around the Winters' living room.

"Where's the aquarium?"

"It split a seam," Sandi said. "Nine o'clock at night and, whoosh, this pane of water curls out of the corner. I'm screaming and Geoff comes running thinking there's a break-in or something. He has me push against the glass to try to slow it down. Ever tried to stop a wave? It ruined our Bokhara rug."

Yes, I could see it was missing too, but I missed the tank. It had been the heart of this room, a refuge where my eyes could stray. I missed the fish too, some of which I'd helped collect. I asked about them.

"The only ones that survived were the juvenile moray and the tomato wrasse. They had dug into the damp gravel while we were mopping up the floor. The kids cried and cried over the butterfly fish wilting away on the bottom. Geoff netted the two survivors along with some wet gravel, drove down to the beach, and tossed them in."

"Couldn't you fix the aquarium?"

"Nah," said Geoff. "We're out of here in six months, why bother?"

"I'll miss our collecting trips," I said. And I knew I really would. Aside from a couple of dives over the reef I'd done with a crazy Italian the first year I was in the country, before I had reason to believe the shark stories, the collecting trips were the only times I got out snorkeling in protective tide pools. It was one of the few things I could do with the Winters where we forgot about work. You just got absorbed in all that marine life out there on the flats. The kids would come running up breathless to show their latest catches. Bright entities of distilled beauty balanced themselves against the slosh of the buckets. At the aquarium, we would watch their diaphanous fins beat in rhythm to their breathing, mouths opening to us in silent song. I imagined the marvel I felt just wandering the tide pools would become overwhelming in a place like the Great Barrier Reef.

I told the Winters I planned on traveling via Australia once my contract was up, do some real diving. Then I added, in a poorly fabricated effort at sentiment, "It looks like our lives here are just about over. You guys get out of here before I do."

"Hey, let me pull some strings, get you assigned to our new post," Geoff said.

He always thought we got along just fine.

"Thanks, but no thanks. You don't even know where you're going yet."

We laughed in about as friendly a way as we ever could. But I was serious. I didn't want another post. I'd spent too many good years in tough countries working for projects that fell apart as fast as it took to turn your back. If I was going to survive the cancer, then I damn well wanted a different life too. This wasn't the best attitude to take facing that last year with the agency. The place was hard enough to work in, and things turned ugly right away.

My head mechanic went over to the oil company. I blew my top at him right in the garage, in front of all his friends. I played it worse than a cranky colonial out of Il Duce's time. Somalis don't take kindly to that sort of thing. Neither do I on my better days, but that day, as a couple of his friends came up to cool me down, I just fired them on the spot. Took weeks of bullshit down at the Ministry of Labor to patch things up, and then I ended up with a couple of extra mechanics who were obvious plants. There went my rapport with the nationals.

You might think that Customs would have had a sympathetic attitude about relief supplies coming into the country, but no. They decided to put a new import duty on all food goods. At first, they toyed with luxury items, which are supposed to be duty-free, like beer and the junk food that went to the embassy commissaries. Most expats had duty-free privileges, so this was a way of casting disapproval on our neocolonial, not to mention infidel, ways. Then Customs figured they'd make more money if they hit up the NGO food shipments too. They held up our containers for more than three months. Telexes flew back to headquarters, the UN, and the State Department. We took letters to all the ministries and concerned officials. Geoff and I alternated days at the port and in the ministries with our appeals.

There had been a time when I'd thrived on that sort of thing. It was part of the romance of working in the developing world, and I had taken a kind of perverse delight in sitting in offices crowded with supplicants. I'd counted the dusty files fading on sagging shelves piled high up the walls and delighted in discovering a lost passport propping up the leg of an official's desk.

But now I couldn't muster any patience. I began to wonder if I had just been denying the stress and strain of it for years. Maybe that had made my body more susceptible to the cancerous bud. An even more obvious reason for it was all this standing around the port in the fierce sun. I began to begrudge any time I had to spend there and became very conscious of any exposure. I ducked into the shade of the warehouses, kept myself slathered in sunscreen, and always wore a floppy straw hat, long sleeves, and slacks in that sweaty heat. What was I doing in this place? Why had I even come back? I was angry with myself and could find plenty to get angry about in everybody around me, too. Geoff wasn't doing his part in negotiating with the ministries. Out in the camps, relief workers weren't rationing food supplies sensibly, so people were going hungry.

In the evenings, instead of eating out at the Golf Club or watching the movies offered at the French and Italian cultural centers, I'd stay in my little bungalow near the heart of town. It was a tiny, whitewashed place with green latticework enclosing the veranda in a pattern the Italians had favored in the colonial days. I'd light a mosquito coil out on the porch, open a can of beer, and listen to the wind play in the neem trees, sinking into the sounds: the muezzin calling from the mosques of Hamar Weyne and the wash of traffic mixed with the crash of the waves on the beach along the Lido a few blocks away. No matter what shortages were in effect, I managed to keep up my own stock of beer and drank just enough to calm me down each night. Nothing was fun anymore except fishing, and I got pretty fanatical about heading out on the water on Fridays, the start of the Muslim weekend. It became my most effective escape.

I'd book the boat as often as I could, enough so my partners were getting pissed about it, but they mostly had families and didn't care to get out as much anyway. We had fixed it up with a Volvo engine from the Swedish fisheries project and used old CIA radio masts for our outrigger poles. Now, nearly all the original partners had gone. As far as I was concerned, it was mine, and I wanted to get all the fun out of it I could before I left. I'd slap on the sunscreen and stuff a bandana behind my big-billed cap, making me look like some wigged-out legionnaire with sunglasses, and I'd hit the high seas. I liked to fish by myself, with Abdi to man the wheel and gaff the fish. This wasn't a very good way to sell my share, but I didn't worry about that until it was almost too late.

One morning, I got up very early to beat the low tide and drove out to our mooring in Gezira, the fishing village on the edge of the coastal dunes twenty kilometers south of town. Bruckner came along. He was interested in buying my share. I was down to six weeks on contract and there were not many expats around who seemed interested in fishing. I wanted to leave the boat in good hands, so I introduced him to Mustafa, who kept watch on our mooring, and Abdi, who was really more of a fishing guide than a boat handler. He fished all week, so he knew where they were running when he'd take us out on weekends. I wanted to be sure the partners kept Abdi on the job because he was good with the boat, and some of them just wanted to party and drink when they got out there on the water. I showed Bruckner the natural gap in the reef where you could get through in just about any weather or tide. Even if you got hung up on the seagrass, you'd at least be inside the reef and could wade in. There wasn't a Coast Guard, so we had had to figure out as many safety measures as we could for ourselves.

The feathers on the lures fluttered in the breeze, ready to be dropped as soon as we got past the reef. God, it was a great day! Just a light swell, the surface glossy and dimpled, and deeper, the water was so clear and blue. We could range out over the horizon if we wanted to, but the dorados were running thick in packs along the reef, and the king mackerel were cutting our bait in two. By ten o'clock, we'd boated three dorados and two kings. One of the kings was massive, five-foot long and heavy, widening past the snaky stage. I figured Bruckner was a sure buyer.

In the middle of all this activity I caught myself wondering if, somehow, my doctors might have missed a cancer cell or two, that one got through and lodged somewhere else. Or, hell, that swarms of them swam on through so at the next checkup the doctor would suggest, after feeling around, we'd better do a biopsy. This put me right out on the Great Barrier Reef again. It would be a lot like this coast actually—the waves dazzling and moving, our bodies tuned to their rhythm, dancing our balance on deck, and shouldering our tanks for the dive. I'd roll off the boat backward, hand on my face mask and regulator, then slowly free fall to the coral plateau and cruise among the canyons, taking in life at its source in this billion-year-old Eden. Sponges and sea fans shaped like submarine cacti would strain for plankton, the very molecules of water crowded with minuscule organisms, and my eyes would brim with the colors of all the circus fish. A school of squid would jet by leaving an ink-black cloud. Well, if it's going to be suicide, I caught myself thinking, then why prolong the bullshit? Why not just shoot and get it over with? I tried to imagine the moment before I would pull the trigger. Life would just brim up inside, buoy me like the dazzling waves and fill me with the sense of being alive like never before. Maybe it was the Dramamine, maybe it was the flashing sun, but for one moment, here and now, I felt what I thought I would only be able to feel at the end, which made me wonder.

Well, Bruckner didn't buy. His wife thought it was too much money. And I'd been straight with him too—spending too much time fishing could cut a real chunk out of a marriage. Bruckner wasn't the type to be worthy of the boat anyway. Nothing out of him but comments like, "Wow, what a monster!" I actually thought I'd rather not sell it at all than sell to a guy like him. I was sour on everything by then.

Work got even worse before the end, crazier. Geoff was gone and the new agency rep foundered in culture shock. Everybody found reasons to be bitchy and cruel, myself included. For a while I thought I would see the new guy get psycho-evaced, but then I wondered if I wouldn't qualify for a medevac ahead of him. I had these aching twinges in my gut—which was no small wonder with all the beer I was putting away. My head skipped to the worst-case scenario: an operation where they'd open me up, poke at my pancreas and liver, then just shake their heads and sew me back together because there would be nothing left for them to do. Of course, Heineken was the only remedy at hand to take the whole thing off of my mind. Work wore me down even more, and I resented what it was doing to me.

It was down to my last week and I still hadn't sold my share of the boat. This new guy, Alex, comes to work for UNHCR and says he's interested. By now we are full into the southern monsoon. The entire ocean starts to flow like a river scrolled with whitecaps out to the horizon, and the fishing isn't even any good. I tell Alex it is rough, but he says he's ready, so we go on out to Gezira.

Mustafa poles us out to the boat in his canoe. Mustafa's

age shows in his peppercorn chin whiskers, white and black. His wrinkled, dark skin is spotted by a kind of fungus that stands out, ruddy brown. I doubt he has traveled farther than a day's walk from Gezira in his long life. He gets ahold of the boat and steadies the canoe so that we can board. He's excited today, but he doesn't know much English, so he waves his free arm out to sea and says, "*Soobaan*," nodding his head, grinning. They've been catching *soobaan* today, dorados.

Alex says to me, "Who is this guy, anyway, Siddhartha?"

I chuckle. I'm beginning to like Alex.

Mustafa is saying one of his few foreign words, which happens to be Italian, but it doesn't take much to figure it out, "*Colosso*." He is raising his eyebrows now and jutting his lower lip toward the breakers pummeling the reef in one huge line of white plumes all the way down the coast.

I point out the tree shaped coral outcrop on the beach, opposite the gap, and tell Alex this is what we get a bead on to guide us in from the outside. And the gap is clear, really clear. Its hundred-yard width shows the only open stretch in the line of billowing breakers. I know it's going to be rough out there. I'm afraid Alex is going to get discouraged and won't buy my share. Abdi takes us right out and I spread a couple lines, but it's hard work with the waves knocking us all over the deck. It'll be pretty crazy if we actually hook a big fish. We head up the coast toward the refinery. The waves are crashing so strong their mist obscures the smokestack and tanks of the refinery. There's a flock of seagulls spinning and working the waves. Abdi heads for them.

We get a strike and I offer it to Alex. He waves me to the rod, because he's not comfortable enough to try taking in a fish. I stumble to the rod and work the fish in fast. It's a small skipjack tuna, its cobalt blue scales mottled to green in the silver by its tail. Nothing fancy, as far as I'm concerned, but I hope it impresses Alex.

We barely start up and there's another strike. Abdi says it's a sailfish this time. I think I see a bolt of darker blue in one of the waves but, hell, they all have umpteen gradients of blue.

I say to Alex, "You take him. Get back by the rod."

He's game now and hobbles to the rod.

Well, the sailfish doesn't hit again, and Abdi tries to head us upstream to chase a flock of seagulls, but we're over the shelf now and huge swells are building up on it to the breaking point. We turn sideways near the top of one and it just shoves the boat back 150 yards. Abdi heads back into them as one heaves up to a sharp crest that's still rising, so he cuts the engine to let us slide over it. I can tell Alex realizes that Abdi knows what he's doing. We come crashing down the other side but could have easily nose-dived if Abdi had kept pushing it. With nothing but angry waves surrounding us, it's going to take hours to get back to Gezira. I don't want to get capsized out here on my last trip. I look over to Abdi.

He says, "We try little one at refinery, eh? We go back to Gezira inside."

"Is there enough tide?"

"Enough," he nods. "Who can stay here?"

The little gap is downwind about a kilometer, so we

bang on over there as fast as we dare. We sluice through the narrow, smooth patch crawling with foam from breakers just to the side of us. They're rolling like lateral tornadoes, gleaming porcelain, but harmless to us now. There's a lot of coral inside the reef and although the water is flat, it is stippled with spiky little wavelets making it difficult to see. Abdi knows this place well. He sits relaxed at the wheel and the rest is a breeze. Alex and I relax, too. We parallel the beach and watch a flock of sheep cropping the fine new grass on the red dunes. They form scattered patterns, bright as beads with their white bodies and black heads. Abdi's little brother is keeping track of them and runs, waving to us. The kid loves to intercept us, loping down the beach to inspect our catch.

Alex tells me about sailing. Ten years ago, he had dropped out of college when he'd gotten busted for trying to grow a little dope for personal use. It got him so pissed off about America he'd skipped across the border into Mexico for a while. After he calmed down, he returned stateside and decided he wanted to learn how to sail. He crewed on an eighty-foot wooden sailboat that was a hundred years old. They went from Key West through the Panama Canal and out across the Pacific to Tahiti. They sailed sixty-odd days, moving slowly at first across dead water near the Equator. Later, in rough weather, they spent the final twenty days pumping the bilge, because they'd sprung a plank. The boat was so crusted and sharp with barnacles, the captain wouldn't let anybody work on it outside in the waves. So they patched what they could inside and pumped, watch after watch.

I look out at the waves breaking on the reef and the ones mounding and scrolling far behind it. This is all familiar territory to Alex, so I know the boat will be in good hands. I even feel a little embarrassed for being so scared out there, but I know we did the right thing. Abdi, Alex, and I all deemed the conditions dangerous. It's okay to be safe and enjoy the smooth ride along the shore. My whole year at work has felt like fighting those waves out there, and I know it is time to leave. I think I'll fly east to Thailand for a long, laid-back vacation. Then I'll skip the Great Barrier Reef and head back to the States.

When I got to Thailand, I visited a temple on a green mountain above the rice paddies of Chiang Mai. You had to climb hundreds of steps to these gentle, old monks who were sprinkling people with blessings, dipping bamboo whisks in a water bowl and swatting fine drops at pilgrims and tourists alike, with a smile. You could shake a numbered stick out of a bamboo vase. There were little, wooden drawers numbered to match the sticks, and they held papers with lengthy fortunes printed in Thai script. If you wanted, you could entreat the Buddha for something while you shook the sticks in the vase. I wanted to know how I would do. Would I survive the cancer? Would I start a new life?

A young guide was translating fortunes for his tour group. I asked if he could also do mine. He studied it and read out, haltingly: "You are a fish in the rainy season.

There is plenty of water. Swim anywhere you like. There is plenty of food in the paddy, too. Be mindful of the dam. Take care not to jump it. Pray every day and wait. One day the floodgate will open. You may then move on."

Breakfast in Bali

Walt Davis sat down at his table in the hotel restaurant feeling just as exhausted as he had on the first day he landed in Bali. In a week of touring he had not found the respite he'd so desperately sought. Instead, grim reminders of Goma popped up daily, parallels unbidden, proffered by Agung, his leather-jacketed taxi driver and spiritual guide to the island. Agung added sites of Bali's mass killings of 1965 to the itinerary and pointed out that the great volcano, which bore his very name, blew its top the same year.

Back in the hotel room, CNN kept up its coverage of the Rwandan catastrophe. It occurred to Walt that he should simply turn off the television, but there seemed to be no stopping the obsessive mode he was caught up in, so why fight it? This was all a part of the process he had to undergo, wasn't it? He shared in the same sort of grief work, as one of the psychiatrists in the camps had called it, that the multitudes were struggling with beneath the Virunga Volcanoes. Walt's private work remained contiguous with theirs, jet lag notwithstanding. Now, just before he descended from his room through the hotel's profuse tropical gardens, CNN had brought Damascene Bucyana's face to him, gloating, spread larger than life on the screen, that split reed in the husky voice so hauntingly familiar as he'd hounded his militias boys to haul away sacks of flour from the back of a relief truck. The reporter matter-of-factly announced that food was arriving regularly overland, in place of the airlifts at the height of the crisis, though its distribution at the camps did not always reach the most pitiable and vulnerable of the Rwandan refugees. A final frame focused on a group of wide-eyed children huddled in the mud. This set Walt's right eyelid to twitching, barely noticeable to others, but evidence of Walt's catalog of serious bodily signals from his conscience.

He scanned the breakfast menu that stood neatly open on the starched, white tablecloth with its setting of heavy Dutch plates and cutlery. There was little choice to make, but he took his time, enjoying the quiet of the spacious room and the sunlight flooding in from the jungle garden in great crystalline buttresses. Ornate pillars crawled with carvings imitating the totemic temple decorations and gargoyles of the island, a testimony to some architect's respect for native culture or, perhaps, to another government-sponsored, labor-intensive sop for local craftsmen. The effect was pleasing, even if somewhat busy. Walt caught the eye of Mas, his young waiter, at the far end of the room and nodded.

Mas shouldered a tray and strolled the length of the room, his face alternately pewter and burnished gold as he passed through the bars of sunlight. With a smile, he presented Walt that morning's offerings: a pot of tea, a hand of miniature bananas, and a tiny flower basket. The basket, loosely woven out of a few pale fronds and laden with frangipani blossoms, was the same as those the ladies of Bali distributed to all the shrines and statues around the island. Walt felt far from incarnate, yet subtly moved to bestow another tip in deference to the cult of the wealthy traveler.

"Good morning, Mr. Davis."

"Morning, Mas."

"What'll you have?"

"A plain omelette."

"Anything else?"

"No."

"Agung is here," Mas said, as he deftly poured tea. "I will tell him you are now eating."

Mas smiled so sweetly it sickened Walt. How could the kid actually be so happy? There seemed to be no falsehood in him; he simply, genuinely aimed to please.

As Walt stirred sugar into his tea, he remembered it was his day for mefloquine. Still in the malarial zone, and occasionally visited by a frisson of latent fever, he would have to continue the course through his first weeks back in the States. He could go back to his room and get the stuff well before the omelette would be cooked, but why bother? Why squelch a good day with the dull headache and depressive funk it brought on? He would take it in the evening with a couple of stiff drinks.

In Goma, he used to take the mefloquine with a big bottle of Primus just to iron out the side effects. But back then, after exhausting days in the camps, they all used to put away those big bottles of beer every evening at the hotel by the lake.

No day had been worse than the day Walt met Damascene Bucyana. Walt had seen the man previously and noted his bumptious personality in the dreary crowds around the food distribution points. But on this particular day, Bucyana and his boys had grabbed three of Walt's volunteers, bound them with sisal cord, and forced the truck driver to haul them all out to the warehouse. Walt had been going over the inventory in the warehouse with his three Congolese staff when he heard shots outside. He carefully edged up to the door to see the truck roll into the compound, overflowing with armed men. Several dropped to the ground still shooting in the air, then took aim at him. He saw Greta, Sam, and Jacques high up on the truck and surrounded by ragged armed men. Sam looked the worse for wear—blood running from his nose, an eye puffed closed. Jacques stood dejected and sad. Greta, defiant, shook groping hands loose from her person.

Bucyana jumped out of the cab, hiked up his trousers jauntily, and strode up to Walt. He let out a hearty, jocular laugh—a laugh that communicated confidence in his control of the situation and, at the same time, seemed to imply it was all a simple misunderstanding that would be quite funny once he explained the particulars.

"Ah, *mon vieux*," he began, in his rumbly Rwandan

French. He introduced himself as one Damascene Bucyana, burgomaster of some town in Rwanda. He explained he couldn't fault these men for taking the rash step of tying up those relief workers, but with the good director's help, he would clarify things to the men so there would be no problem. He spoke affably, even though he stopped a good five feet away from Walt, flanked by a couple of his armed cohorts.

"And what problem is that?" Walt asked.

"You see, this truck unloaded all of its precious cargo at the Tutsi camp. There was nothing left. These men want to be sure that the rest of the food in the warehouse goes to their wives and children. They've seen two truckloads given to the *inyenzi*, the cockroaches, as they prefer to call them, and they are worried nothing will be left."

Walt mustered his most authoritative French and said, "We have developed a fair and balanced distribution list. You have nothing to worry about. There will be plenty of food for all concerned. However, I must ask you to release my workers, immediately."

"Oh, I do not command these men. I come as a translator because they do not know French, you see. I am a facilitator, if you will."

"Well, tell them."

Bucyana tossed a few phrases back to the men, his voice at once wry and risible. There were a couple of chuckles in response, making it clear that not everyone needed a translator. One fellow, next to Jacques, took up the game and shouted back a couple of words in Kinyarwanda. The group tightened up around the hostages. A machete rose slowly behind Sam's head like a flat horn and stayed silhouetted there.

"He says you must open the big door."

"I'm sorry, but I can't do that."

"Perhaps you do not comprehend this situation, *Monsieur le Directeur.* These men will stop at nothing. They come from fighting the enemy in a devastating war. They are desperate. Their children and their wives are dying of hunger. The lives of a few white strangers mean nothing to them before such a great hunger. Be wise, *Monsieur*, or you will regret this silly show of stubbornness."

Walt knew he had to accede, but he hardly believed the fools would actually kill his volunteers. Yes, they were among the killers—the craven men who had slaughtered hundreds of thousands across the border—but this, right here, was all a big bluff, surely, so why not make it awkward for them? There had been a few incidents of this kind recently and no foreigner had been hurt. But there was always the possibility of a first time, and looking up at Greta and Sam and Jacques, he knew he would never be able to forgive himself if any further harm came to them.

He stood his ground for a long minute. Then, just as he was opening his mouth to say, "*Comme vous voulez,*" the men tumbled off the truck and surged to the great warehouse entrance. Damascene Bucyana's lieutenants eased themselves into positions surrounding Walt. A Congolese staffer at the lock pushed the crowd back with his shoulders while he manipulated the key, cussing at the lot of them to wait before they ruined the doors. The doors swung free and they all rushed forward to the towering piles of sacks. Yellow pallets full of cooking oil caught the eyes of some who raced to rip the plastic bottles free of their binding.

Damascene Bucyana marched one of his lieutenants, who boasted an AK-47, to the entrance and let the machine gun rip overhead. Puffs of flour formed a cloud above the sacks near the roof. The silence that followed was broken only by the soft purr of beans pouring on the floor as the men stood still, Bucyana sorting them for various tasks: some to climb the sacks and toss them down, others to shoulder them out to the truck. No one was to touch the oil, though several dared to whine until it was made clear, even to Walt, they were going to be coming back for all of it.

Looking at Damascene Bucyana's back, Walt studied the workings of his left shoulder blade beneath his sports coat, picking the precise point, just under the blade, where he would aim his first shot. He would use a .50-caliber machine gun—the type favored by technicals in Somalia—mounted on his getaway pickup and jerk the burst to the right to be sure the spine would splinter after the heart was ripped to shreds. Once Bucyana dropped, he would take out as many of the rest as he possibly could and, like a wily gunslinger, attack the armed ones first to make his killing score more efficient, though certainly not effective enough with the guys still behind him on the truck blasting his body and brains into a bloody oblivion.

It was in that moment, shaken by the awful will of his own imagination, that Walt had to accept the end point of his thirty-year commitment to pacifism. There wasn't time to sort out the personal consequences or mourn this change in his view of himself. But it was all too clear to him that at this point, he would readily and willfully kill. And he seriously wondered if he had come to this simple insight too late.

Just then the truck backed up to the entrance and he was urged to move aside, a gun barrel bumping his skull under the left ear. Greta, Sam, and Jacques were being led to the office door and Walt was pushed in their direction. Inside the office, one of their captors grabbed the tiny Motorola security net radio off of Walt's desk and banged it hard on the edge. Then he thought better of his action and pocketed it. There was little else of interest, because Walt did most of the paperwork from his room at the hotel. Walt was asked to take the seat at his desk and then his arms, pinched together with coarse cord behind his back, were tied to his chair. Greta and Jacques were pressed into the two other chairs and Sam was shoved to the floor. Two doors—the one they'd come in and another opening on the storage area—were shut. Not long after, keys were shakily turned in each.

Walt could only see out the office window at a high angle, so he had to guess at what was happening outside. As the loaded truck rumbled out of the compound gate, he heard his Congolese staffer curse, then start to yell. A burst of gunfire rattled against the siding at the far end of the warehouse. It seemed the man was being executed. Walt could see some men riding atop the sacks in the truck. They slapped their hands down on their thighs, laughing as they swayed with the load. Afterward, in the quiet, there were sounds at the end of the building: a few bumps against the siding as remaining militia men positioned themselves to drag the body away from the building. Then there was a hoot—probably a reaction to some unexpected tremor from the body, or a spill of bodily fluids, which then brought them laughter.

Greta began to sob, her shoulders shaking in sharp jerks.

"Why the hell do they have to kill him?" Jacques snapped.

"To keep our truck driver quiet and on the job for another load," Sam said.

"That's all?"

"Maybe they just didn't like him."

Someone banged on the aluminum walls to quiet the talk.

"Quiet!" Walt whispered. "Or we could be next."

They sat quite still, minding intimate strategies for survival. Walt looked at Sam's battered face. His lips were caked with blood and two or three teeth had been knocked out of the right side of his mouth. Now and then he would lean forward with gently puckered lips to let another drop of clotted spittle fall.

Another phase in the life of the camps had begun, possibly a deadly phase for relief workers. The world-be-damned, deeply anarchic streak of the refugee leaders just might see advantage in scaring off relief workers, who were indeed unwelcome witnesses in the camps. Yet surely, this Damascene Bucyana would not want further attention drawn to himself by killing foreign relief workers. Killing

Walt's local staffers and pillaging warehouses would serve terror well, for now.

Walt found this thought reassuring somehow. It calmed him of the fear that had been building up in him—the disquieting fear of unpredictable, brutally inflicted pain and slow death. He tried to gather the calm into his face, to better calm his young volunteers. Greta's eyes were red with tears. He met them with steadiness and a firm nod to instill confidence. She sniffed bravely and tossed her bangs out of her face, straightening her shoulders as best she could. Jacques kept his frightened eyes to himself, gazing at the laces of his boots.

To keep his worst fears at bay, Walt busied himself composing points in his head for a fax to the regional office in Nairobi: warehouse sacked, Congolese personnel killed, an American bloodied, all held hostage. New security measures a must or all relief efforts will be jeopardized.

Burnout had driven many workers away already. He recalled the attrition rate at the onset of the exodus of refugees, with the cholera and the piles of corpses along the roads, the stench, and the ubiquitous cries of orphans. New workers arrived, got sick to their stomachs, and turned around, begging for passage out on the next empty cargo plane. With this present, extreme breach of security, how could the relief agencies go on? How could the safety of volunteers be guaranteed? How could the agency ask them to serve? A difficult moral question must be faced: were our efforts fattening up the killers at the expense of the refugees and better supporting their return to war?

After these musings, Walt wanted to add his request for

leave to the fax. He would hold that for later, but leave was finally beginning to make sense. He had been ready to take home leave in March but postponed it to make a quick trip to southern Sudan. For the past two years he'd been serving at the regional desk in Nairobi, mostly occupied with Somalia. In April, the catastrophe struck in Rwanda and he felt he had to stay on. He had come to Goma in May to survey possible sites for camps. He'd secured this warehouse on the edge of town, pre-positioning some food and plastic sheeting. He had even made arrangements to hold a couple of rooms at the hotel by the lake, away from the hubbub of the town, where his workers might rest. At the time, the hotel had been almost empty, testimony to the moribund Congolese economy. He'd returned to Nairobi to monitor things when the flood of refugees engulfed the town overnight. He felt he should have better prepared the groundwork somehow, but no one could have imagined the scale of the exodus. Postponing leave yet again, he flew directly to Goma to serve on the spot. Now, with hands numb behind his back, a hostage in his own warehouse, who could fault him for taking leave, if indeed he were to survive the day?

After some time, three trucks accompanied his project truck back to the warehouse. They were huge trucks belonging to the defeated Rwandan army. Uniformed soldiers showed considerable discipline as they filled their trucks with loot. They did not bother to reload the project truck. As the last truck revved up to leave, Damascene Bucyana unlocked the office door.

In the finest of francophone turns of phrase he said, "I

am quite desolated to see that you have been subjected to such awful treatment by these men. Rabble, you understand, beyond my control."

With a gracious smile, he turned and headed for the truck.

"That's a shitty alibi," Sam sputtered. "Won't hold up against our testimony in any war crimes tribunal."

Bucyana waved from the cab of the truck as it rolled out of the compound, flashing his gloating smile.

"I'm going to kill that bastard!" Walt growled.

The words came out of Walt before he could stop them. His volunteers stared at him, stunned at his vehemence. In all their arguments and debates over beers and suppers at the hotel, he had been the most adamant in his defense of non-violent approaches to conflict resolution. He had been almost comical in his knee-jerk reactions against exasperated calls for armed guards at delivery points, or the exercise of capital punishment on the most obvious of war criminals. His record of service had given him a kind of unquestionable authority—alternative service in Biafra during the Vietnam War, when many of the Goma volunteers were yet infants. Then he'd served in Bangladesh, followed by two stints in Ethiopia, and then Somalia.

The tone in his own voice startled him. But he refrained from any corrective rephrasing, any softening of his vow.

The driver stepped into the office and bent down to untie Sam.

"*Ça va?*" he asked. His right ear sported a bloody cauliflower.

"*Pas mal,*" Sam nodded wearily.

Once they were all freed, Walt had Greta accompany Sam to the truck. Walt and Jacques took a quick scan of the warehouse to assess the losses. Walt retrieved the keys which still hung in the office door keyhole and, with Jacques's help, locked the warehouse doors. None of the Congolese staff were in sight. He sent Jacques to join the others at the truck. Walt walked over to the side of the building where he'd heard the shooting. A short distance away, out among the weeds on the edge of the compound, he saw bodies sprawled on the ground. Three. Flies had already found them. He couldn't stomach going over there and reaching out to check them for pulse. Instead, he took a moment of still, close watchfulness using the gaze he had practiced with anxious loving care as a young father, when he would peer in upon his sleeping children to make sure they were still drawing breath.

That evening he wrote his fax to Nairobi and included a request for home leave to be granted as soon as they could bring in someone to take his place. He walked it over from his bungalow to the main building where a communications room had been set up by the press and relief agencies. There had been only one fax machine in all of Goma when the crisis broke, so an expensive satellite telefax had been brought in and set up among interested parties. Nairobi received his fax on the third try. Then he headed out to the terrace where Ray Burnham, an old friend from his Ethiopia days, said he would meet him.

He quietly sipped a beer, alone at a table. High up in the night sky there was a dull red glow, diffused in the clouds but flat and even at the bottom, delineating the rim of Nyiragongo Crater. Recent eruptions had left huge black lava flows walling the countryside into savage fiefdoms. Even the hotel stood on an old flow. At the water's edge, where Walt often took early morning walks, he could see the abrupt inward turning of the flow as it had come into cooling contact with the lake. Now it provided a pretty set of little curling cliffs and mysterious underwater caverns in the clear green waters for curious, snorkeled tourists to explore. But the nightly glow of Nyiragongo cast a menacing air over the sprawling camps, where it served as a favored endgame image for the evangelists who worked the misery of the people there. The apocalypse had already visited these people. It was men like Damascene Bucyana who rode the livid sky as its horsemen, terrorizing the masses with radio lies into heading straight for Hell, and then bullying them into staying there to resurrect the Hutu army of Armageddon.

But this condemnation was too one-sided. Walt had monitored the other side of the story, beginning three years prior, when Tutsi rebels started the war. They too were said to have committed atrocities: villages aflame in the night, flows of refugees in the thousands rushing down the hills, and women impaled live on crude stakes. Evil took sustenance from all sides. In the lulls between battles, acts of terror were never claimed for attribution, in order to better terrorize and manipulate the population. Who could bury a grenade triggered to a hundred-franc note next to a school yard? Who could possibly think of killing twenty-one children in that manner?

Strangely, immersed as he had been throughout his adult life in the world of refugee camps and those fleeing from violence, Walt realized he had remained a willful innocent. Yes, he had known in his heart of hearts that he was fully capable of violence. In his adolescent soul he had committed himself to pacifism in a kind of existential leap of faith. He had come to believe he could thwart the power of evil with his own good works, his agnostic realism perversely mirroring the values of his rejected Protestant upbringing. But over the years, all these high-blown abstractions had come face-to-face with the hard knocks of life. Though he had worked for years amidst the cries of starving babies, it was not until the birth of his own first child he could hear the deep personal sorrow calling in them. Their cries had simply been irritating, grating, overwhelming to the ear. Suddenly, in clearly recognizing the rich and eloquent timbre of his daughter's individual cry—her call to him distinguishable from all others—he began to fathom the depth of sorrow and personal terror in the cries filling a camp dispensary. It was the kind of feeling he had to numb to keep functioning professionally, but it was there to be heard when necessary.

A whole world of trouble and irretrievable loss had come to this place and he could not help but feel it in himself. Alone on the terrace overlooking the calm lake, silver and smooth in the moonlight, the voice of his daughter, now fully grown, rose to him in its wrath. The richness in her voice lilted above the first word in a kind of primal descant, colored with the timbre of her earliest cries in infancy, "Daddy! Don't you get it? You're to blame. You left us! How can you ever expect us to want you back?" This, nearly three years ago, when he'd stopped at her college for a surprise visit sandwiched between the home office and his next posting. And it was true, he had left them during that long second stay in Addis Ababa—left them for a young Ethiopian beauty, in a spate of straightforward, sexist, racially exploitative, midlife bullshit. And when his head had cleared, the nice house and gardens were empty, free of their playful voices and the voices of their friends from the International School. Nancy had taken the children with her back to the States and there had been nothing but alimony to pay ever since. Where would he go for "home" leave? To whom could he go? She had the house in California. A furnished apartment outside the beltway would have to do, with nothing but cable TV to keep him company.

He was in this frame of mind when Ray came to join him out on the terrace. "My God, Walt. Let me get you another beer."

"Do I look that bad?"

"I'll say."

"It comes from having murder on one's mind, Ray. I would have killed a man today if I'd had a gun. I mean blast the sonofabitch to smithereens."

"No fun being tied up, eh?"

"It's more than that, Ray. It was in my gut. I really wanted to kill him. I still want to kill the bastard."

"This isn't the old bleeding-heart Walt Davis I knew in Addis."

"We live and learn."

"Well, I agree with the live part. I'm not so sure about the learn thing."

"I've watched guys like him get away with shit for years. In some countries they're just bureaucrats who manage to skim off most of the food bound for relief. Other places, they do more blatant stuff. The Khmer Rouge praying on refugee camps. The Serbs. I'm tired of them getting away with it. And no tidy little report of yours or any other agency is going to stop them, Ray."

A waiter brought over fresh bottles of Primus and a glass for Ray.

"Thanks for the vote of confidence," Ray said.

Walt immediately felt the fool for ranting as he had. Ray Burnham had come down from Geneva to do a quiet, preliminary survey for the potential of setting up a war crimes tribunal.

"Sorry."

"No problem. And you're right, a lot of them do get away with it."

"Well this one won't. I swear if I see him again, I'll blow him away."

"Hey, hey. Just keep a file on him, Walt. Discretely. Six months from now we may have a tribunal in place."

"Fat chance. But I suppose you're right."

"Suppose? Walt, don't tell me I have to convince you."

"That's just it. I lost my pacifist stance today. There's only one way to really put a stop to these guys. Forget the supposed effects of the court of world opinion. Doesn't phase them."

Walt drained his glass and topped it up. He topped up

Ray's glass too, shaking his head at himself for pitching this fit.

"Ray, I've got home leave coming to me, but nowhere to go. Never did buy a place after Nancy took the house."

"Ah, I see. Well, don't rush back to the States, then. Take the long way and stop for a while in Bali. You deserve it. Shouldn't cost you much over your travel allotment."

Ray talked it up: the temples, the dancers, and the artists. This idyllic island consecrated to art and pleasure. Never having been to Indonesia, Walt found the idea appealing.

Nairobi informed Walt that it would take three weeks for his replacement to arrive. Things deteriorated dangerously in the camps. Walt was drawn into more regular and uncomfortable dialog with Damascene Bucyana, who had indeed begun to take on an obvious leadership role in the rump government's attempts to co-opt the distribution of donated food. Walt kept his eye on him and documented any moves that could, in any way, be registered as evidence of his complicity with the killers. But what was worse, Walt found himself entertaining other, devious plans—perhaps he could offer the man a pack of cigarettes laced with poison when he came to sign for a truckload of food or, maybe, he could have somebody plant a land mine in the path of his truck. The plans were idiotic, but the violent impulse behind them continued to bother Walt. It goaded him to document the man all the more. He directed oblique questions about Bucyana to fellow relief workers, UN personnel, and reporters.

Then, one day at the dispensary where Sam and he were delivering a shipment of medicines, he caught Bucyana at his game. Bucyana was just leaving the dispensary, shaking hands with a Swedish doctor, laughing in his jocular way. He nodded to Sam and Walt as they passed him, carrying their newly delivered boxes of meds into the tent. At the far end of the tent, a young girl stood vigil over her father, who lay on a cot with his head wrapped in gauze. A male Congolese nurse was still cleaning and dressing a gash on the man's right arm. Walt left his box with Sam and asked him to bring in the rest. He walked down to the cot and asked the nurse who had done this.

The nurse cautiously motioned, with a slight jutting of his jaw, in the direction of Bucyana, who was by then walking out to his Land Cruiser.

In French, the nurse said, "He's paid this man a visit, the better to convince him."

"Of what? That it's actually safer to stay here than to return?" Walt said, tartly.

The nurse's eyes darted around the tent. Then, when he'd assured himself no one was paying attention, he allowed himself a grim, shaky little smile.

The man's daughter was no more than ten. It was clear she was the only surviving relative to accompany him to the dispensary. Walt couldn't bear to look into her eyes. He took out his notepad and asked the nurse quietly if he would be willing to share details for the documentation of this case.

"On Bucyana? Only anonymously."

"First, just to be perfectly clear. This was the work of Damascene Bucyana?"

"Yes, done at his command."

"I need the name of the victim."

The girl shook her head. She knew some French, it seemed.

"For now," the nurse said, "why not just give the date and the location of this dispensary unit. You can see the number on the bed for yourself."

As Walt wrote it down, the girl cleared her throat to get his attention.

"Leave," she said. The look in her wide eyes had such great force, Walt took a step backward. He tucked his notepad into his pocket and left to chat with Sam and the Swedish doctor outside the entrance.

The next morning, the bodies of the girl, her father, and the nurse joined the rows of corpses lining the highway to await mass disposal. The Swedish doctor delivered the news to Walt at the warehouse around noon. He advised Walt and Sam to get back to their hotel. He had already informed the UN Command, and they were likely to have some additional instructions for Walt.

An American military officer pulled up to the hotel in the early afternoon and informed Walt that he had twenty minutes to pack his things. He and Sam were to be flown to Entebbe Airport on a military transport flight that would leave within the hour. The UN Command did not want to take any further risks.

Walt had little to pack. He made sure his notepad and

documents on Bucyana were safely tucked in his briefcase. As the C-130 roared off the tarmac, he had the unremarkable intuition that all hell was about to break loose in the camps. At least he would not have to be there to deal with it. The plane climbed high over the lake and then swung up between the sharp, blue-green peaks of the Virunga Mountains, revealing the incredible beauty of the landscape, devoid of any sign of human misery. Then, the edge of Walt's eyelid began to dance its silly jig high above the dwindling forest home of the mountain gorillas.

Agung announced the morning's itinerary, the Barong dance, as Walt took his seat in the tiny van. He drew a last toke from his clove spiked cigarette and politely flicked it out the window. "Barong is one big tiger dragon. Very beautiful. You will see. Much better than the *Kecak* dance."

"Lead on, Agung."

Walt had rather liked the *Kecak* show. At night, by torch light, a great wheel of men, seated bare chested round a tiny center stage, had chanted and waved their arms in unison. Some had wrapped their arms in intricately woven patterns around the central players. Others had waved their hundreds of hands with splayed fingers, beseeching the lovely couple, pulsing with desire, a warm-blooded sea anemone filtering the surrounding spiritual sea in order to draw great power to its heart. They'd formed a living mandala in the torchlight, chattering, *"Kecak! Kecak!"* with insistent, primal energy. It had been an energy quite infectious, yet inaccessible to him. Those imploring hands had reached out all too much like the hungry hands of refugees.

"Traffic busy. Always busy in Denpasar. We go slow today."

"Too much exhaust, Agung. When will you guys start some pollution control?"

"Ha! No problem. Good rain cleans every afternoon."

"Yeah, well it's making me dizzy."

"No problem. We take nice country roads today."

The diesel fumes sickened him, and those country roads curving sharply around the hillsides, echoing the contours of the rice paddies, did little to settle his stomach.

Walt felt a quiver of fever work through his back muscles. He knew he would have to be sure to take his mefloquine when he got back to the hotel. With a little luck and the diversion of the Barong dance, he'd weather the day somehow.

"Barong good for you. Every time make me feel better," Agung said cheerfully.

They rode in silence until they reached tourist buses beached among a huddle of hotel minivans and *bemos*. The temple grounds had been well modified to accommodate the tourist trade which, by all the evidence, was booming. Agung flashed a set of tickets at the entry and led Walt into the courtyard, which was well shaded with canopies to protect the tourists from the hot sun. The gamelan orchestra was set up alongside the cement dance floor, ready to accompany the dancers. The musicians all wore long-sleeved batik shirts with designs busy as snakeskin. They were already devotedly plunking away at an amazing array of gongs and xylophones.

Soon enough, the mighty Barong stepped down the gateway to the stage, his terrible tantric eyes framed in an elaborate crown swirling with golden flames. Great fangs curled up to his cheeks as he smacked his wooden jaws and wagged his spangled tail, which followed him around on a wobbly set of second legs. For all his fierceness, he seemed most like a friendly puppy. Of course, he was supposed to be sympathetic, because he was on man's side. Agung explained this as the battle heated up between Barong and Rangda, the wicked, fire-breathing witch so ready to destroy the world. As Rangda rallied, kris dancers raced to support Barong, but Rangda made them turn their wavy knives against themselves. Barong magically kept the kris knives from piercing the skin. Wild, maniacal expressions contorted the men's faces in agony as the knife points pressed up sharp folds of skin. Suddenly, it was all over, with jubilant gyrations on the part of the kris dancers as they opened the way for an old priest's wife to come forward on stage, holding up what seemed a tiny, pale ball of fur. With the flick of a wrist, she beheaded a chick, its body tumbling to the stage floor, where weak wings worked to spill what little blood the bared neck could offer for the expiation of any lingering sin.

It was more than Walt could stomach. He stood up angrily amid the applause to leave the performance, but Agung tugged him back down.

"Best part is coming," he whispered.

"But why kill the little chick for a tourists' show?"

"Not a show, Mr. Davis, the real thing. We must always make sacrifice, or the masks lose their power."

Walt's eyelid began to twitch as he reluctantly waited for the next act.

The stage was swept clean to make way for a pair of lovely, young dancers who tilted their floral tiaras with exquisite poise. Their wide eyes darted dramatically in synchronous wonder, while their hands deftly described an utterly new world. This elaborate, clean-limbed grace soothed Walt's anger and disgust, charming him to stay.

Now he began to appreciate Ray Burnham's advice. This was the Bali he'd meant for Walt to see. His rapt pleasure in the dance left him light-headed, almost high, when he finally stood up to follow the horde of fellow tourists out of the temple grounds.

Agung took him on up the hill to the painters' town of Ubud. Walt wended his way through the galleries, soaking up the quiet stillness of the place. Few tourists had bothered to visit the town that day, and he was glad to have it nearly to himself. The jungle trees of the town crept through gallery windows, where all manner of paintings told tales of maidens bathing in jungle streams under ruined temples. There were bright epics of the Ramayana and the Barong ogling village crowds in courtyards surrounded by the interlocking branches and flowers of the forest. He immersed himself in the cool of these galleries, hoping to lower a rising feverishness that seemed to have come to stay.

His strength failed him, however, as he stood before a painting that was specifically historical in content.

Throngs of Balinese in a coastal forest faced off against a high masted Dutch ship, cannon balls flying mid-air. Though some were fighting off attackers on the beach, others behind them had turned their kris knives upon themselves and were falling forward in a heap of jumbled limbs, committing a kind of mass suicide that Agung pronounced *puputan*.

Before Agung could steady him, Walt slumped to his knees, dizzy and faint.

"You okay, Mr. Davis?"

Walt nodded. There was a hint of clove on Agung's breath as he gently placed his cool hand to Walt's forehead.

"Hot! Hot! Mr. Davis. We must get you to hospital."

"No, take me back to the hotel, Agung. I just need my malaria medicine."

"You sure?"

"Really, I'll be fine. Just let me rest a bit."

The gallery owner rushed to them. He spoke worriedly with Agung in their strange language, then called over to the clerk who brought a bottle of mineral water. It was refreshingly cold. Walt slowly gathered his wits and stood up, leaning heavily on Agung's shoulder. The clerk offered a shoulder too, and the three of them made their way out to the van.

Walt clutched the cold bottle to his chest and closed his eyes against the dizzying ride to the hotel. He woke from a doze, shivering as they pulled into the parking lot. Mas and Agung helped him up to his hotel room. He showed them the mefloquine and downed a double dose.

"I'll be better by morning," he said to them.

Mas stood with Agung at the doorway and said, "You want something to eat?"

"Are you kidding?"

"I'll come before dinnertime, see how you are doing."

"Thanks. Thanks a lot, guys."

He lay flat on his back for hours, his head growing much too heavy to lift under the lethargy of the fever. A wakefulness kept him from sleep, induced either by the mefloquine or the fever itself. Perhaps it was a bit of both. He felt absolutely wrung-out, yet positively alert.

As the room grew dark with the night, the alertness brought with it a vivid dreaminess. At first, this was pleasant. He revisited the dance of the two girls and their lovely crowns of blossoms. He loved the way their wide eyes rolled in unison. Though they did it mechanically, almost like the moving parts of a mask, they seemed to nonetheless project a mysterious kind of power: a power to delight demons and charm monsters, a power to stave off evil. And this brought him up short, because the eyes radiated the same power of the ten-year-old girl standing beside her father in the dispensary in Goma. It was as if she were looking out from their faces, and they were all accusing him.

He woke up sobbing. The girl had lost her life because of his foolhardy campaign to get Damascene Bucyana. And Bucyana had won! The only bit of difference Walt had made was that three more people got killed in the camps. How would he ever get over that fact? How could he continue to live with himself? With a fever as strong as this one, maybe he would not have to endure himself for long.

In the darkness he could view his body as if from above, and it was a kind of living map of the world, where two puzzle piece countries stretched him wide in a tug-of-war around the equator. Bold lines—red, green, and orange—showed the rivers, roads, sea lanes, and subterranean fault lines where the lava glowed between the cracks, revealing great tectonic presses below the tight boiling skin of the Indian Ocean. The two countries were his hands: Rwanda, the right, and Bali, the left. It seemed they were vying to be declared the best place in the world. The winner would rule a tourists' paradise and the loser would preside over Hell. Gold veins of lava raced along his arms to feed the royal volcanoes of the lands, brimming, bursting their tops to flow in burning rivers down their slopes, chasing the miserable hordes before them to their doom in the steaming seas. If he could only cool down his very skin, he might save them.

"Mr. Davis," Mas called. "Mr. Davis! Oh, you burning!"

Walt could barely recognize his worried face.

"I make cold bath for you fast."

Effortlessly, Walt found himself swaying high above the earth, cozy as a little child in his mother's arms. But then, he was tottering out over the brink of yet another catastrophe. Mas nearly lost his grip as he practically tossed Walt into the tub and the cold water brought the fever down with a splash.

Mas dampened a washcloth and spread it over Walt's head. He knelt next to the tub and gravely dipped his fist into the water from time to time, to trickle more drops onto the cooling cloth. It took a while for Walt to realize he was completely naked. His body, pale and covered with dark woolly patches and trails of hair, must have made him look like a hairy monster in Mas's eyes. He'd blacked out, no doubt, while Mas drew the bath.

"You are pretty strong for a little fellow," he said to Mas. "Mighty strong to lift a guy like me."

"Nah," Mas muttered bashfully. "Danger make me strong."

"To save a life, my friend."

Walt studied the stolid severity of Mas's face, trying to get him to meet his eyes and accept his thanks. Gradually, ever so shyly, it shone through, that golden smile.

Walt spread his fingers before him, turning his palms inward, then out. He wiggled his fingers as if he were at a keyboard.

"Does this hotel have a computer I can use?"

"Sure. IBM. Macintosh. We got everything."

"And a fax machine?"

"Yes, Mr. Davis. What you thinking? We not modern?"

"Sorry. I just want to send a fax to a friend of mine in Geneva. Finish up a bit of business."

"Business? You on vacation. You sick with very bad fever. Forget business. I call doctor now. You rest."

Walt lay back in the cool water listening to Mas talk to the doctor over the telephone. That singsong voice recalled the sound of fountains Walt had seen when Agung had taken him to the temple spring at Tampaksiring. It was a very old place of healing and rest that he knew he had to visit again. Carved stone spouts fed squared pools, where swans drowsed in the rooted shade of banyan trees. Mandarin koi cruised green canyons of tattered algae, while a dragon eel elegantly unfurled its regal length beneath lily pads and lotus.

ACKNOWLEDGEMENTS

With the publication of *Nestlings,* I have been able to bring Paul's lifelong goal of being a published author to fruition. I could not have done it without the help and support of many friends along the way. First of all, I wish to thank my dear friend Joyce Danielson, who coedited the book with me and retyped the manuscript. Without the teamwork and support she provided, her experience living and working in Africa, and her meticulous research skills, this book would not have come together in the way that it has.

To my sister-in-law, poet Eleanor Bowman, and friends Jackie Newlove, Laurel Pollard, and Ellen Abrams, my thanks for reading and commenting on different versions of the stories. To Paul's "Congo brothers" Gordon Anderson, Alden Almquist, and Ted Ericson, thanks for your readings and comments and for your friendship through the years. And to the alumni of The American School of Kinshasa (TASOK), many of whom read and commented on the story "Nestlings," thanks for continuing to be my extended family.

To my wonderful daughter Lena Olson, who is so like her father in her intellect, interests, and passion for writing, thanks for your love and support and for keeping so many family memories alive for me. I am so proud of you!

And finally, to Jamie Rath and all of the editorial staff at Outskirts Press, thanks for your help with the design and production of this book.